A Borderline Freaks MC Story

Borderline Freaks MC #3

MariaLisa deMora

Edited by Hot Tree Editing

Proofreading by Whiskey Jack Editing

First Published 2019

ISBN 13: 978-1-946738-48-6

DEDICATION

How important it is for us to recognize and celebrate our heroes and she-roes! ~ Maya Angelou

To my readers who are current and former servicemen and servicewomen. Thank you.

Contents

One 1

Two 11

Three 19

Four 39

Five 49

Six 59

Seven 69

Eight 81

Nine 95

Ten 109

Eleven 113

Twelve 117

ACKNOWLEDGMENTS

A certain selflessness surrounds the kind of dedication that is key to signing on the dotted line, and willfully giving away years of life to defend our country against threats both foreign and domestic.

In the face of adversity, they persevere, and we are the better for it.

That should never be entered into lightly, and the commitment of those individuals should never be taken for granted by those of us who have not served in those capacities.

You have my gratitude, everlasting.

Woofully yours,

~ML

Lack of In-between

Wolf finds Rose harbors more secrets than he expected, and the deeper he pulls her into his life, the more he likes it.

Once a man's been embedded in the bloody aftermath of battle after battle, with no relief in sight, he's forever changed.

Wolf came home from overseas to find his world askew. He was no longer a husband, since he and his ex agreed they were better friends than partners. But he still held the coveted position of father, an experience so confusing and rewarding it sometimes left him breathless.

He's got a lot on his plate personally, and even more with the Borderline Freaks and the challenges he and his club brothers have hit lately.

He just doesn't have time to make room for a relationship.

Right?

One

Wolf

Paul Bailey sighed as he turned back to the party. Colleen was already walking off, which was fine, their conversation was over. Just because he and his ex-wife could be friends didn't mean she was his favorite person. Her arrival had been a surprise, and once they'd finished chatting, she'd apologized for coming out uninvited, but he'd agreed with her, the information she brought him couldn't wait.

Their daughter had just turned twelve and was struggling with nearly everything in her life right now. School, volleyball, the divorce—Erika couldn't seem to find a path through the changes, and he'd had to watch her painfully floundering more often than not. A suspension from school, though? That was new and troublesome. Paul would meet Colleen at the school Monday morning to talk to the vice principal and see what kind of light he could shed on the situation.

Paul, or Wolf as the men who surrounded him called him, scanned the crowd. The Borderline Freaks MC, the motorcycle club of which he was a member, was throwing its annual pig roast, celebrating the anniversary of the chapter's charter. The evening was still in the first, milder stages of the party, the part where kids ran around underfoot and outsiders dotted the ranks of the members. Those hangarounds might one day become an FNG, or fucking new guy, then move up to probie, and eventually member. It was the path many of the men who wore the patch had taken, including Wolf.

He couldn't find the face he'd hoped for, so he looked through the throngs of people again, slower, intent on each woman until he'd eliminated all of them. Not a one was the redheaded firecracker with soft curves he was certain had been here a moment ago. Rose Bronson, a waitress at a local diner, friend to his brother Blade's old lady, and the woman he was hoping to continue to woo tonight. *Goddammit.*

Blade's old lady stood, and he watched her greet Blade wordlessly, then follow the man around the clubhouse towards the parking lot. They were apparently bugging out early, which was annoying. Not that he begrudged his brother having found his match in Jenn, but he'd wanted to pry info on Rose out of her.

With a shake of his head, he stalked towards Monk, whose head was bent over his phone as it so often was these days. Monk's current obsession was texting a war widow he'd met while on a BFMC run a couple of years ago. Something in the woman had resonated with him, and Monk had kept tabs on her since, even meeting with her at her husband's grave. Wolf and Neptune had a running bet going on how long it'd take their brother to grow a pair and ask the woman out. So far, all their expected time frames had been well exceeded, and Monk wasn't pushing any boundaries. *Yet.*

"Brother." He greeted Monk and got a quick grin and head nod in response. "How's Amanda today?"

That smile turned upside down, and Monk scowled. "Why do you assume I'm texting Amanda?"

"Aren't you?" Head tipped to one side, he waited.

"Well, yeah. But that didn't answer the question, man." Monk's chin lifted, and he seemed genuinely annoyed.

"Brother." Wolf clapped a hand on Monk's shoulder, digging his thumb in deep enough to feel, but not enough to trigger the brachial nerve cluster. "While you've set the land-speed record for a tortoise race in romance, when you're grinnin' like a fool at that damn phone, odds are it's Amanda on the receiving end of whatever you're tappin' out." He shrugged then lifted a hand, rubbing fingers and thumb together. "I'm all about that easy money, and you're a sure bet."

Monk relaxed slightly and raised a shoulder in embarrassment. "Pegged me. Fuck you, brother. It's disconcerting how much you see."

"It's why y'all keep me around, and you know it." He gestured towards the clubhouse and the parking lot beyond. "Blade already skip out and head home?"

"Yeah, had something to do at home." Monk's grin returned, quirked to the side with wicked humor. "Someone to do, I mean. He's happy. Never thought I'd see him like this again. Glad for him, you know?"

"Yeah, it's good. I don't think any of us expected him to bounce back so fast."

Monk's face twisted. "Fast is a relative term. Man went through hell after wrecking out."

"He did. No argument from me there. Good thing you were there to help him through."

"We all helped him, wasn't just me." Monk's phone dinged, and his entire expression lightened as he glanced at the device. "Amanda wants to go riding. I'm gonna bail, brother."

"With good reason, my friend. Go make that pretty lady smile." He lifted a hand, and Monk gripped his wrist, pulling him in for a one-armed clinch. "Ride safe."

"Always do."

Monk was walking away before Wolf remembered he'd been going to ask about Rose. *Dammit.*

An hour later and the vibe of the party was beginning to change as families left and single women turned up looking for a good time. It said a lot about the Borderline Freaks as a whole that women in general felt safe enough to come and play. Wolf scanned the available fresh faces and sighed. None of them were what he was looking for, through no fault of their own. Too young and he'd find himself doing a mental calculation of the age difference, not only between him and the chick rubbing up on him, but between them and his daughter. *I'm getting old.* A flash of red in the corner of his eye caught his attention, and he snapped his head around to stare at the woman hanging off Neptune's arm, head back, laughing. Not Rose. *Dammit.*

Hands shoved in his pockets, he traced the outline of the key ring holding his bike and house keys. Each side of the flat disc was engraved with a short phrase, scratched into the metal with the tip of a knife.

He'd sat at the counter of the diner and watched Rose wrestle with the tiny thing for more than an hour, not knowing what she was doing. In between customers, she'd retreated to a tiny booth and resumed her efforts, head down, flaming hair falling around her face in curtains as she unfolded a tiny pocketknife and tapped or poked at the metal laid flat on the table. When it appeared next to his plate mixed in with his change, he'd nearly missed it, the surface catching his attention because it was different from the coins. He'd flipped it back and forth between his fingers as he walked away, reading the front and back again and again.

Ride free.

Be safe.

One was part of a mantra he had tattooed along the underside of one arm: Ride free or die.

The other felt like a plea, something a woman would say to her partner before he rolled away balanced on twos. Something he'd never gotten from anyone but his brothers before. Colleen hadn't worried about him on the bike, their marriage dead in the water long before he'd joined the club.

By the time he'd realized what it was, he'd been out of the diner already. When he looked back through the plate glass windows, Rose was standing behind the register, and she'd lifted a hand to wave. He'd almost gone back inside, would have if she hadn't whirled and dashed into the kitchen. Running away as clearly as if she'd held up a sign stating her intended avoidance.

Wolf had gone home and drilled a hole in the disc that night, attaching it to a ring and swapping his keys over. Now, when he handled his keys, he remembered that instant of wonder when he'd read the words the first time.

His next trip to the diner had been equal parts intriguing and frustrating. While he'd clearly been seated in her area, she hadn't served him and quickly disappeared, the other waitress rolling her eyes when she first approached his table. Distracted, he hadn't even glanced at her as he ordered, then looked up and asked, "Where's Rose?"

Another eye roll, then, "She's busy."

He'd looked around the diner, where only a handful of tables were occupied. "Uh-huh." Wolf considered his options and decided to go for direct instead of beating around the bush. "Give her a message for me when you take my order back, okay?" The waitress had already taken a couple of steps away, but she'd paused at his words and looked back at him. "Tell her thank you, and that I'll do my best."

Since then, he'd had exactly zero chances to talk to her. Seeing her at the party tonight had his chest puffing out, imagining she'd come to be with him. Only now she was gone without a word, with scarcely a shared glance between them.

"Penny for your thoughts?"

He turned and looked down at the woman who'd approached him. Pretty, but young. So damned young. Blond, not redheaded. Blue eyes, not green. Whipcord thin, not curved for days and made for his hands.

Wolf smiled and tipped his head, indicating a group of men just up the way who were already eyeing the young woman. "They'd be better company tonight, darlin'."

Her bottom lip pushed out as she pouted prettily. "I saw them." She paused and fluttered her eyelashes coquettishly, something he didn't realize he detested until he watched her do it. "I came to you. I like my men with some experience under their belt." Her hand lifted and rested on his arm, and the wrongness of it all struck him so he shook her off and stepped backwards, away from her.

"This is me trying to be polite." Lifting his chin, he indicated the parking lot. "You might be better served by looking elsewhere entirely, if you won't take rejection well. BFMC men aren't famous for our kindliness."

Her mouth flew open, then shut, and she stared up at him. Without moving. He sighed.

"If you won't take your leave, then I will." Tipping an imaginary hat to her, he sauntered off. "See ya."

On the bike and in the wind, he let the events of the night wash away, his attention focused on the machine he rode, the light traffic, and the shadows along the ditches that could contain deer or other wild critters. An hour passed, then two, and he realized he'd circled back around and was on approach to town via the highway that ran in front of the diner. On impulse, he pulled into the lot, and somehow he wasn't surprised to see Rose's car parked in back.

Stepping off the bike, he stretched as he looked into the front windows of the diner.

Rose was watching him.

If he stretched a little more than was absolutely necessary, he'd never admit it.

LACK OF IN-BETWEEN

Two

Rose

"Oh my Jesus."

It was only when the customer's voice faltered and paused that Rose knew she'd spoken aloud. She blinked hard and tipped her chin down, smiling at the couple seated across the table from each other. She recited their order, finishing with, "Did I get everything?" When the husband nodded—Rose thought they were married, or at least the woman was, because she wore rings while the man's fingers were bare of ornament—Rose flashed them a smile as she turned to walk away. "I'll get this put in for you and be right back with your drinks."

She hadn't quite made it into the kitchen when the outside door whooshed open, bringing in the smell of the woods, motorcycle exhaust, and something she'd come to know as uniquely Wolf. One hand on the in-passage door, she paused and glanced at the man who'd just walked inside. His form was tall and broad, his shoulders filling out the leather jacket he wore so well. Wolf was a member of the Borderline Freaks MC, a local biker club that did a lot to disrupt the media's depiction of what a club more typically was. The jacket wasn't a fashion accessory but a necessary part of everyday attire for this man. Until he stretched like he had a few moments ago, the jacket and shirt under it riding up to reveal a broad strip of skin above the waistband of his jeans. Then it was as revealing and enticing as a full-monty show. That had been what drew her attention away from the customers.

He'd been coming to the diner for months now. Rose had been working the first time the BFMC had made a stop for food, but another waitress had served his table that day. Rose had found her gaze returning to him repeatedly throughout the time the club members spent in the diner, then had stood at the window and watched while he mounted his bike and rode away. It wasn't until he'd turned back to the building and given her a wave goodbye that she'd embarrassedly realized her interest hadn't gone unnoticed.

The next time Wolf came in was only a few days later, and she hadn't been quick enough to hide in the kitchen. Rose knew her cheeks had been red when she took his order, silently rebuffing his attempts to engage her in conversation. That had only seemed to increase his interest in her, and Wolf had taken to coming in every few days. He'd park and then pause before entering, apparently verifying which section she was working. Once inside he'd slide into a seat where she'd have to wait on him, that grin he always wore growing wider at her stammered words.

Now, Wolf cocked his head to one side and, smiling, asked, "Everything okay, Rose?"

She realized she'd been frozen in place, hand on the door, eyes on him. *Oh my Jesus*. "Right as rain, Wolf. Take a seat anywhere. I'm by myself tonight." Which meant there was no chance of foisting her table off on another waitress, just to keep temptation at bay. "I'll be right with you."

Pushing into the kitchen, she paused just inside the door and let her lungful of air out in a long exhale. Just being in the same room as that man had her ovaries working extra hard to talk her into jumping his bones. He was everything she'd ever wanted in a man. At six foot four inches, he still loomed over her taller-than-average frame by six inches. The man was confident, former military, able to hold his own in a conversation with a variety of people—and kind.

So kind, even when he thought no one was looking.

She'd watched him hold the door for an elderly couple one night, then learned later from friend-and-fellow-waitress Jenn that he'd paid for their meal, too.

It didn't hurt that he was easy on the eyes, too, the scruff on his jaw lending him an air of authority she'd often imagined carried through to the bedroom. Oh, and her imagination hadn't stopped there, bringing her night after night of steamy mental images in her dreams. Hot, fit, sweet, and seemingly in pursuit of her. *It doesn't matter what my body thinks.*

She forced herself to remember what she'd seen earlier tonight, a truth about Wolf she hadn't wanted to believe.

Safely seated on the picnic table bench with Jenn, Rose had looked around the crowd of partygoers, trying to find the one face that had driven her to finally accept the oft-extended invitation to a BFMC blowout.

She'd wanted a chance to get to know Wolf in longer than three-minute conversations held over the passing of plates and glasses. Had hoped to find out more about the man and see if the reality matched her mental image. Instead, she'd seen a gorgeous blonde walk up to him and be met with wide-open arms, the kind of greeting reserved for someone loved. Rose had forced herself to watch a moment longer and saw his head dip towards the woman. Not needing to see more, she'd dragged her gaze away at that movement, made her excuses to Jenn, and fled. On her way home, the waitress on shift at the diner had messaged her with an urgent request, and so here she was. And now, here Wolf was, too.

Handsome, kind, generous—and so very taken.

"Order in," Rose called out to the cook, and stuffed the ticket under the clip. She scanned the kitchen but could see no good reason to delay going back out into the dining room—and Wolf's table.

Drinks in hand, she made her way to the table where she'd just taken the order, depositing them with a smile. On her way to Wolf's table—she sighed when she saw the man had taken a seat on the far end of the diner—she detoured behind the counter and grabbed a glass of water and pot of coffee. He already had the ceramic mug upturned and ready when she got to the table, so she poured his coffee first.

"You can't be hungry after that pig roast," she teased, and immediately could have bitten off her tongue. *Way to broadcast you were there, idiot.* Maybe she could distract him from her slip. "Did you want some pie or anything?"

"Why'd you leave?" Wolf sat back on the bench and slung an arm across the back, his fingers dangling off the edge and dangerously close to her hip. Rose took a step away and froze when Wolf's eyes narrowed at her movement. "You were there, and then gone."

She swung her empty hand out, indicating the diner, hoping he wouldn't ask if she'd already been scheduled. "As you can see, I'm working."

His chin tipped up, and he stared at her with an intensity that mesmerized her. The rumble of his words flowed over her, leaving gooseflesh in their wake. "There, and gone, and not a word to your friends."

"I told Jenn." She shook her head, trying and failing to find a smile. "She's the only one I knew there anyway."

"Lies. You know me." His fingers twitched, clutching at the air almost as if he wished she were within reach. "I looked for you."

Rose finally was able to summon a smile as she shrugged. "Didn't realize I needed to telegraph my movements to the masses." Going for a laugh, she pulled her mouth to the side in a pouty grimace. "I'll do better, boss man. Promise."

She sighed with relief as he seemed to accept the words at face value, grinning up at her as he teased, "See you do."

"So. Pie?" She nodded at the glass case on the counter behind her. "Chocolate pecan is a favorite of mine, but the lemon meringue is good, too." She patted her stomach in a self-deprecating move she regretted immediately, not wanting to seem to flirt. "I can attest they're both delicious."

Wolf moved, leaning towards her, and Rose held her breath. His hand landed on her waist, then swept down her hip, the tips of his fingers sliding along the outside curve of her ass. It was an intimate touch, something she didn't expect, and heat flared between her legs, desire curling in the pit of her stomach. "If the pie is part of what helps keep you in these gorgeous curves, I'll take one of each and you can help me eat them." His gaze held her pinned, stuck in place as if she were physically tethered to him.

The ding of the cook's bell, along with his bellowed, "Order up," broke the tableau, and Rose whirled away, fleeing Wolf's table wordlessly. It took two trips to deliver the couple's order, then a third to refill their drinks.

She took the coffee carafe with her when she returned to Wolf's table, topping off his cup. "Did you decide on the pie, Wolf?"

"No pie, not this time. Sit a spell with me, Rose." She tipped her head to the side, lifting one eyebrow. He proved he could read her expression when he said, "Not that puzzling, honey. You're not busy, and I like to chat with ya." He shrugged. "Sit a spell."

"I shouldn't." *I can do this. I can be friendly without flirting.* "But a couple of minutes wouldn't hurt anything." She slid into the seat across from him. "Did you stay at the party long? It looked like it was going to be a fun time."

"Not too long. Blade and Jenn took off after you did, then Monk had to leave." He lifted his mug and sipped, blowing across the hot surface. The movement of his lips was hypnotizing. They were full and looked the mix of perfectly soft and masculine firmness. He smiled, then licked along his bottom lip, and she clenched her internal muscles. *Oh my Jesus.* "Got tired of standin' around by myself, so I went for a ride."

She blinked, then lifted her eyes to meet his. *Why would he be standing by himself?* Rose nearly blurted her question, clamping her lips together at the last moment, staving off embarrassment by a nanosecond. Avoiding the alone part of his statement, she latched on to the other. "Where'd you ride to?"

"Not every ride has a destination." He glanced out the window, and she followed his gaze to his bike. It was big and black, intimidating even from this distance, the tiny seat for passengers looking like a joke. "Some of the best days are spent on two wheels, going wherever the wind takes me."

"And you don't worry about gas or bathrooms?" Laughter bubbled out of her. "I'm such a control freak. I'd be a nervous wreck at the end of that kind of day." She caught a glimpse of the dining couple's reflection and noticed they were nearly done with their meals. "I should get back to work." Standing with a muffled groan, she arched her back to ease the aching down low, by her hips. "Want another top-off?" She offered the carafe, following through when he nodded. "Thanks for the chat, Wolf."

"Paul." He reached out, the backs of his knuckles grazing across the back of her hand. "I'd like it if you called me Paul, Rose."

Grinning broadly, she nodded. "Okay, Paul Rose it is."

His laughter followed her as she walked away.

Three

Wolf

He studied Rose as she interacted with the other customers, taking their empty plates, balancing the pile deftly as she dug in her apron pocket for their check. She'd handled him just as easily, he realized. Even through the short conversation, she'd avoided any personal revelations, and he really knew no more about her now than before.

While he knew more coffee at this hour was a bad idea, he had a deep unwillingness to leave yet. In a few minutes, the other people would be out the door, and he'd be alone out front with Rose. He finished his coffee and set the mug down with a clunk just as headlights swept the front of the diner. Squinting into the brightness, he watched as the van maneuvered around, finally backing into a spot on the far edge of the parking lot. *Odd.*

Rose's laughter caught his attention, and he glanced over, watching as she joked with the couple while she made change, then ducked her head in thanks as she placed a small wad of bills into her apron pocket. The man's gaze connected with Wolf's, and they offered mutual nodded greetings; then with an arm around the woman, the man steered her to the door.

He didn't know why, just something stirring in his gut, but it said to keep watching, so he did. The man had opened the passenger door of their car, standing close to the woman, when the van's lights flicked back on, spotlighting the couple in the bright glare. Wolf saw the van begin to move and was up and over the counter a breath later, wrapping his arms around Rose as he took her to the floor with him, twisting in midair to land on his back, then twisting again to put his body between her and the front door. They'd hardly stopped moving when he heard it, a sound he'd never gotten used to, even when it was part of the everyday cacophony of noise.

Pop. Pop, pop. Pop.

Measured and deliberate, this was a marksman squeezing off as few rounds as were needed, not playing Hollywood stuntman and spraying the entire front of the building.

An instant later, the plate glass in front of where he'd been sitting exploded, shards recoiling off the wall at Rose's back and cascading down around them.

Pop. Pop.

Louder, the shots were nearer the building now, and he could hear the echoes bouncing off the surrounding woods. Rose was breathing heavily, her face tucked against his shoulder, eyes squeezed tightly shut. Wolf heard the cook cursing, but the sound was growing fainter, likely as the man moved farther away from the front of the building.

Pop, pop, pop.

A beam of light appeared on the wall behind Rose, van headlamps providing proof of passage through the counter for a bullet. The shots were getting closer, the shooter having moved to fire through the empty window towards the most likely hiding place.

"Rose." He breathed her name, lips pressed to her ear. She startled, and her fingers tangled in the front of his shirt. "When I say go, I want you to crawl into the kitchen. Be careful of the glass, but go as fast as you can."

Her response was scarcely audible, but he heard the murmured, "No," as she shook her head.

Pop.

"Yes." He pushed the word out between gritted teeth, because another beam of light shone through the counter overhead. Gravel and glass ground underneath someone's foot, and he knew the shooter was likely looking for an angle where the counter wasn't protected by the outside wall or booths. It's what he would do. "On three." Wolf pulled in a deep breath, filling himself up with Rose's scent. "One." He pressed a kiss to her temple. "Two." He released her and reached for the gun nestled in a holster on his six. "Three." He pushed Rose away and rose on his knees, gun preceding his body as, with his other hand, he deliberately knocked a row of coffee mugs off a shelf and away from the kitchen door.

Pop.

From behind him, he heard the ratcheting slide of a scatter gun being racked. He glanced over his shoulder to see Rose on her ass next to the kitchen door, shotgun in hand. Her face was pale, features twisted in a combination of rage and fear. *Jesus*.

A metallic clunk from inside the window area sounded, and his mind drew the comparison immediately: a gun being laid on a hard surface. *They're climbing inside*. Within a split second, he'd evaluated what was known—vehicle, one shooter—and what he could extrapolate—single individual attempting entry—and stood with a fluid movement, gun leveled at the booth where he'd been seated only moments before.

A dark figure sat in the window opening, arm outstretched for a gun laid flat on the table. The van was jammed against the couple's car. He didn't see the couple and had a faint hope they'd avoided the crash that had mangled the open passenger door. The van's passenger door also hung open, and he saw another dark form behind the wheel.

Wolf squeezed the trigger, aiming at the table next to the gun. With his trajectory, the bullet would likely skip off the surface and out into the darkness. The bullet dug a furrow in the table, spraying plastic splinters and debris up into the figure's face. A scuff of shoe sole just behind him indicated Rose was on her feet, and not anywhere near out of the line of fire. *Dammit woman.*

"Come on." That shout was from the driver of the van. *Male.* The shooter twisted and leaped off the wall, crying out as they landed. *Also male.* Wolf squeezed off another round into the darkness, incentive for the now-limping shooter to stay on the move. He couldn't shoot the van from this position without going through the glass on the door, and there was too much risk of a ricochet back inside the building where he and Rose stood.

"I don't have a clear shot." Even as he ran the scenario through his head, Rose came to the same conclusion, her voice carrying a tone of frustration. "White cargo van, no rear windows, no company logo. No front plates."

Wolf kept part of his attention on Rose, listening to her clear description of the vehicle with a sense of wonder. He'd honestly expected her to go through the door as told, not take hold of a gun herself and stand beside him. A little pissed she hadn't done what he'd wanted—and a lot impressed by her courage—he stood shoulder to shoulder with her as they watched the van back away from the car, shooter installed in the front passenger seat. Both figures wore face coverings and hats to hide their identities. The shooter had been medium build, unremarkable. Wolf winced when he heard a distinctive metallic crunch just before they changed gears.

"You okay?" He didn't look away from the van, disappointed when they pulled out of the parking lot in a fashion that denied him any glimpse of the license plate. Tires barked on the highway as they roared away, headed out into the country.

"Yeah, you?" Her question was crisp, voice strong.

Wolf saw movement in the couple's car, two heads tentatively appearing from beneath the dashboard. "You wanna make the call and I can check on them?" He gestured towards the booth table where the shooter's gun still rested. "Gonna leave that as is. Long as we don't let anyone near it, I'll count it secured until the cops get here."

"Okay." When he looked at her, she was staring out the window where the van had disappeared, shotgun gripped in one hand, down at her side. Anger had won the battle and was evident in her clenched jaw. "Motherhumpers shot up the diner."

He wanted to grin at her creative language, but his gaze latched on the floor just beside her. Red was puddling out from under the door. "Shit." He lunged for the door and shoved, but something was blocking it from the other side.

Wolf put his shoulder to the surface and pushed hard, only gaining a couple of inches.

"Here." Rose's voice came from beside him, and he looked up to see her grip the frame of the out-door and pull, swinging it wide. She blocked it open with the side of her foot, and he moved past, automatically going to a crouch as he ensured the room was clear of action. A man lay on the floor just behind the in-door, slumped to the side, head hanging loose on his neck. "That's not Gary."

"Gary?" He reached out and laid two fingers along the man's pulse point, digging deeper when he didn't feel a steady thump. "He's dead."

"Gary's the cook. I don't know this guy." She moved away, and the door thudded against his hip. "Hey, y'all okay?" Indistinct voices responded to her, he assumed the couple from the wrecked car. "Okay. Just stay where you are. We'll call the police and get help. Keep pressure on it." Heat hit his back and he looked up to find Rose hovering over him, trying to get a look at the dead man. "Nope, I definitely don't know him. The woman out front got hit, sounds like it's not serious." She dug in her apron pocket and pulled out a cell phone. Tapping on the screen, she stared at it for a minute, then lifted it to her ear. "Dale's diner. Someone shot up the place. We've got a 10-109A and 10-109D." She paused, but before he could wonder at the unfamiliar codes, she nodded. "Correct. One walking but injured, and one dead."

The back door opened and Wolf lifted his gun, aiming it steadily at the chest of the man who entered.

"Whoa, whoa, man." The man waved his arms madly, but Wolf realized he wasn't armed at the same time Rose identified him.

"That's Gary."

"Get down," Wolf ordered, and the man sat where he stood, legs folding up like pretzels. "ETA?"

"Three minutes." Rose's delivery was less crisp, and he looked up to find her staring down at him. She visibly swallowed, and her voice shook when she said, "You could have been killed."

"Hey." Wolf stood and turned, reached for her as she stumbled into his arms. "We're okay. We're both okay." They stood like that until the ringing doppler of sirens became audible through the dampening quiet of the trees. "We're both okay." Her head moved across his chest as she nodded. "Gary's okay." Her laughter was wet and broken, and she moved to rest her cheek against him. "Bad guys ran away."

Though her voice was muffled by his hold, he still heard the pride as she said, "You reacted fast."

"So did you." He angled his body back as he lifted his head to look down at her. "That thing with the shotgun, not what I expected."

"Motherhumpers shot up the *diner*."

The sirens cut out suddenly, and he heard tires on gravel. "They did." He shifted them so he and Rose could look out into the parking lot. When two of the four cops approached the front door of the diner with guns drawn, he was immediately aware that he and Rose were both still armed. "Don't shoot." He reached to the side and laid the gun on the counter. Rose stepped away and did the same; then, wordlessly, they both walked towards the other end of the counter, hands held at shoulder level. "There's another employee in the kitchen, unhurt. And the dead guy in the kitchen, identity unknown. As far as we know, it's just us three in here, and those two." He indicated the couple already walking towards an ambulance that had just rolled in on the far side of the lot.

The next two hours were draining as he recounted the event multiple times, once for each time it got bumped up the chain of command. Rose stood a few strides away, doing the same thing, and Gary sat at a booth in the undamaged section of the diner, presumably doing the same. The major interviewing Wolf shook his head as he glanced over Wolf's shoulder. "You probably saved her life."

"I got the feeling Rose would have been just fine without me."

"And maybe without you, it wouldn't have happened at all." Wolf glanced at the cop walking up and noted the lack of insignia before he recognized the face. He froze as he stared at the man. "Everyone around here knows the

Borderline Freaks are bad news." It was one of the prospects who hadn't made the cut weeks ago, acting out of order at this very diner before threatening Blade's old lady and earning the club's unflinching hatred. The man hadn't mentioned anything about having been a cadet at any point, and surely had not been a state trooper at the time. Wolf knew that for a fact. That meant the man had jumped from the outlaw side of the tracks to the law-abiding in a fast minute. Or had lied to the men he claimed brotherhood with. *More proof the asshole was never meant to be a Freak.*

Anger simmering hot inside him, Wolf clipped out, "Couldn't get a real patch, so you found a badge to hide behind?" Wolf turned and faced him squarely, hands loose at his sides. "And look, you're still an FNG no matter where you go." He peered around the man, scanning the rest of the faces. "Where's your BFF? Don't tell me you broke up already?" He tsked softly. "Bummer for you."

The major stepped up beside Wolf, staring down his nose at the obviously new trooper. "Nobody called for you. Get back on patrol."

Glaring at Wolf, the man nodded, sketched a halfhearted salute, and mumbled, "Yes, sir."

They watched him walk away, crawl behind the wheel of a dusty patrol car, and accelerate recklessly out of the parking lot.

"I'm guessing there's a story here." The major stepped out in front of Wolf, turning to face him. "That man's already a pain in my ass, and he's on thin ice anyway. We're his third troop posting since he finished training and qualifying, something I understand he barely passed by the skin of his teeth. I get the feeling his initial posting had to be desperate for bodies, or the man's kin to someone I don't know about, because he's not a good fit for the job, far as I can see." He shoved out a hand. "I'm Doug Putnam."

Wolf gripped and shook, giving the man his club name, as he'd already provided his government one. "Wolf. He gonna be a problem for this investigation?"

"Depends on what your history is with him." Doug shook his head. "But I hope not."

"He wanted to prospect. We determined he didn't have the correct values to wear our patch, so we removed his name from consideration. Him and another guy were buds, and we caught them harassing a waitress here." Wolf gestured towards the diner. "Released them the same day. Woman they weren't taking no from is now the old lady of a club member, so you can see where the bad behavior won't be forgotten soon."

"Sheee-it." Doug dipped his chin to his throat, studying the ground between them. "His bud got a name?"

"I can get it for you." Wolf paused. "You got any idea where shitstain was about three hours ago?"

"I do not, but you can bet your ass I'll be locating that information first thing." Doug clapped Wolf on the shoulder. "Oorah, Marine. Glad you made it through another firefight unscathed."

"Same, brother. Same." He glanced across the lot. "Can't say the same for my bike."

Two wreckers had shown up; one already had the couple's car attached and ready to go. The other had parked next to his toppled bike, knocked to its side when the van backed into and partially over it. The two drivers were arranging straps to lift the damaged bike to the flatbed for transport.

"Sucks, man."

"Yes, it does." He sighed. "They're going to take it to my shop though, so at least there's that."

"Your shop?" The cop glanced at him, and Wolf nodded.

"Bailey's Builds, out on Central." He didn't even try to stop the way his chest puffed out. "My shop."

"Nice. I'll stop by next week, take a look around." Doug took a step away. "You need a ride somewhere?"

"Yeah, but I—"

"I'll be your ride." He turned to see Rose approaching, purse in hand. "My car's behind the diner."

Doug ceased to exist in that moment. Rose had taken her hair down from the tidy bun she wore when working, and the curls flowed to her shoulders, ends curving around the sides of her throat. He looked closer and saw her smile was strained, lines on either side of her mouth.

"You okay?" He reached for her, surprised when she dodged his hand. "Rose?"

He lost sight of her green eyes, that auburn hair hiding her face for a moment. "Yeah, I'm okay. They cut me loose a few minutes ago. I'm ready to go, if you are."

"Yeah." He paused. Something wasn't right. This was a different vibe from her than a short time ago, when he'd found out how well they fit together, her body against his. Sure, it might have been a comforting hold for both of them in the moment, but simmering underneath had been the knowledge that this was the woman he was interested in and would be pursuing. "Rose?"

"Uh-huh?" She tossed it over her shoulder, not slowing down as she strode away from him.

We'll be in her car in a minute, and she can't run away there. "Nothing. Thanks for the ride."

She pointed her keys at a car, and the lights blinked as she unlocked it. "No worries, Wolf."

He waited until she was inside and buckled to correct her. "Paul."

"Right." Pulling up to the edge of the parking lot, she glanced in each direction, then at him. "Which way?"

Without hesitation, he tipped his head to the right, away from town and home. Maybe driving awhile would give him a chance to figure out what had changed.

Wordlessly, she angled the car up the highway. He saw her adjust her grip on the wheel, and a moment later, low music swelled, blocking out the road noises. "How far?"

"Four or five miles." That'd put them on a parallel country road, which would take them over to another small highway, that would, in turn, lead them back into town. He lifted a hand and fiddled with the radio knob, lowering the volume. "What branch were you in?"

"Huh?" She glanced at him. "Oh, Air Force. Security Forces." She stared out the windshield, that tension returning to her face. "I've been out, DD214, for three years."

"Where were you deployed?" He shifted, settling his shoulders against the door so he could better watch her.

"Op Enduring Freedom. ILO to a Marine patrol there." Her hands moved back and forth across the top of the steering wheel, gripping to white-knuckle intensity before releasing. "Years and miles ago."

"Military police, that's a hella job. ILO, that means it wasn't a permanent posting, in lieu of, right?" He watched a muscle tick along her jaw as she nodded. "I was a scout, predominantly recon. We depended on our SF folks a lot. The job isn't just ticketing speeders on base anymore."

"No, it is not." The finality in her voice lent weight to her brief statement. "I'd prefer to not discuss it, if you don't mind."

"I don't mind." He did, but that line of questioning could wait. There were other, more pressing areas to question. "I like you." Her head whipped to the side, and she stared at him, whites showing all around her eyes. "Watch it," he cautioned, and she looked back to the road, correcting their track, which had been about to lead to the ditch. "I don't know how to state it plainer than that. I like you, and I'm interested in you." He leaned closer and lowered his voice. "Romantically." Wolf was near enough he heard her breath catch in her chest. "You do it for me, Rose. And I want to get a green light from you to see where this goes." He settled back, shoulders against the door again. "I'm getting mixed signals from you tonight, and I wanted you to know where I stand."

"You wanted me to know where you stood?" Her eyes flicked sideways and back front.

"Nope." He smiled as he corrected her. "Where I stand, present tense. This is me right here, right now, talking to you about the current situation."

She didn't respond, and beyond indicating when the turn was coming up, he didn't, either. His statements stretched out between them, and the tension grew as he waited for her to react. They'd reached the other highway, and she laughed softly when he had her turn right again, creating the third leg of the box route back to town.

"What?" Not trying to deny the intentionally circuitous route taken, he shrugged, arms folded across his chest. "I wasn't ready to go home."

"You could have just said so. I'd have driven around for a while if you needed me to."

"Wasn't a need, Rose. Was a want. To spend more time with you. That was my want." His gaze fell on her chest, and he watched her breasts rise and fall as she pulled in a deep breath. *Killin' me, woman.* "Thought it was easier to beat around the bush a little."

"You consider earlier beating around the bushes?"

She gave that soft laugh again, and it went straight to his dick. He shifted in his seat, adjusting his stiffy. "Rose," he began, but she cut him off with a brusque headshake.

"I saw you tonight." Wolf opened his mouth, but she barreled over him. "At the cookout. I went because I hoped I'd see you there. True statement. I've enjoyed our talks at the diner but wondered if there might be more. Thought I'd get a chance to see if I was there and you were there, and we had a chance to talk."

"If you'd stayed, I'd have made that happen. I saw you, too. Saw you when you walked in, but by the time I had a chance to go find you, you were already gone." Stretching out a hand, he ran the backs of his fingers along her arm. "Why'd you leave?"

She shivered and moved her arm away. "I *saw* you." She repeated herself, special emphasis on the verb.

"If that was the reason you came, then why would it make you leave?" Wolf was getting annoyed. None of this made sense, and he really liked things to make sense. If Rose was interested in him, and he liked Rose, then why would she go out of her way to come there only to avoid him? "Help me understand."

"The blonde."

He stopped his head jerk in midmotion, unable to control the startled reaction entirely. "The blonde?" He was wracking his brain for what she meant and finally remembered the party girl who'd driven him away from the clubhouse and party. "Jesus, Rose. Not only was she too young for me, but I turned her down flat." Something struck him then, and he asked, "How did you see that? You'd already left well before she showed her face."

"Oh, no. I was there. I saw her and saw you. It's okay if you're taken, Wolf, but I can't do that to another woman. I can't be the one behind the door." She stopped the car, and he saw they were at a deserted four-way stop. "Which way, Wolf?"

"Left two blocks, then right." She wasn't making any sense. He decided to restate what he felt was already obvious. "I'm not taken, Rose. I'd never play games like that. I wouldn't care if you were there or not, the answer to her was the same. A flat turndown from me."

"It didn't look like a no when you wrapped her up in your arms." She made the second turn, taking the corner fast, her jaw doing that clenching thing again.

"When I what?" Wolf glanced up to see his house approaching. "It's the white ranch on the left."

Rose pulled into his driveway and slammed the gearshift into park, whirling to face him, anger and unexpected pain in her expression. "You were all lovie-dovie, Wolf. It's okay, it's not like we're anything. And," she straightened her spine, shoulders shoved hard against the seat, "it's not like we'll ever be anything."

"Dammit, woman, what the hell are you talking about?" He reached for her, and she slapped his hand away. "The hell?"

"Get out." She held his gaze, those lines of strain deepening again. "Get *out*, Wolf."

"*Paul*." He didn't mean to roar, but everything about the past twenty minutes was confusing and he just wanted one damned thing from her. "See me, I'm sittin' right here. I'm *Paul*."

She stared at him for a long minute, then twisted and put her hands back on the wheel. Voice quavering, she softly repeated his name. "Paul." Then she took any solace that provided, ripping it away. "Get out."

"Rose." Head shaking back and forth, she slipped the car into reverse. "Rose, just give me a minute." When her only response was to drop her forehead to rest on the top of the steering wheel, he decided to give in, for now. "Okay. I'll get out, but this isn't over. I want to understand what I did, and what you think you saw."

"What I *think* I saw?" The laugh she offered was thick with unshed tears. "Nice one."

"Give me your phone number at least." He dug his phone out and accessed his contacts, opening a new record and waiting. After a moment she rattled off the digits, and he input and saved it, then sent her a text. "I'll be in touch, Rose. Tonight was a lot to take in. A lot to get through. Call me, okay?"

She didn't move, didn't respond, and he finally opened the door and slipped out to stand next to the car.

Wolf watched her drive away, that excessive speed coming back out, tires squealing as she made the corner at the end of the street.

She didn't look back.

LACK OF IN-BETWEEN

Four

Rose

She was nearly home when she heard the buzz of an incoming text. The phone was buried in her purse, so she ignored it for the next few minutes. Once home, she backed into the garage and sat in the car, watching the door slowly lower in front of her, the door jittering in tiny fits and starts until it was fully closed.

Even then she didn't move. Hands at ten and two on the steering wheel, she let the events of the evening replay through her head. Noticing the van as she rang up Tom and Barbara's bill. Not that they'd eaten in the diner before, but she'd overheard them talking to each other and noted the names.

Her therapist called it hypervigilance. Rose just knew if she stayed watchful, she felt more in control.

The engine finished cooling before she was able to force herself to unlock the car doors, the slowing ticks of contracting metal silenced. The overhead light had timed out long ago, leaving her fumbling along the side of the car in the dark, feeling her way.

She rounded the bumper, and the lights of the van speared her in the eyes, the roar of its engine growing louder as it raced towards the diner. Rose flung up her hands in defense, contents of her purse scattering as she dodged to the side. A moment later, she lowered her arms and opened her eyes to see the tiny motion-controlled nightlight plugged into an electric outlet next to the door. "Christ on a crutch."

Rose stared down, cataloging the items on the floor. The one thing conspicuously absent was her phone, and she checked to find it was apparently the only thing that hadn't been thrown from the purse when she reacted. Her finger touched the screen, waking the device, and she saw more than twenty missed texts and calls.

Shaking her head, she shoved the phone into her apron pocket, only then realizing she'd never removed it after the diner. Stooping next to the car, she shuffled and duckwalked around, gathering up her belongings and shoving them back into the purse. Bent over as she was, she received the vibrating alert of additional texts against her belly, flesh cringing away from the constant rattle.

Inside the house finally, she toed off her shoes and put them into the closet before taking off the apron. Phone retrieved, she locked the door and made her way to the bedroom. A glance at the clock had her gasping, because she'd no idea it was so late, after three o'clock in the morning, but a quick check of the phone showed it wasn't wrong.

Methodically she removed her makeup in the adjoining bathroom, showered quickly to wash away the stink of fear-induced sweat, and redressed in her pajamas. It wasn't until she was crawling into the bed that exhaustion hit her, making every movement harder than it had to be. Under the covers, she turned to her side and unlocked the phone just as another text came in.

The calls and voice mails were all from Jenn, so she shot off a quick text response that they'd talk tomorrow. *Today, I guess.* She shook her head.

The first text from Paul had come in only moments after she'd been successful in evicting him from her car. It was a brief demand that she let him know when she got home. The next couple were an attempt to set up a date, and she swiped and deleted those quickly, hating the hollow pain that speared through her chest. *I told him I'm not interested in being with a cheater.* She skimmed through the next dozen, which were ever more irate requests that she check in with him.

Rose rolled her eyes and pulled up a response. She'd gotten about halfway through a brief and highly edited message when another text came in from him. ***Jesus, Rose. Tell me you're home safe. Answer me, please***.

A fist pounded on her front door, and Rose rolled out of bed, landing on hands and knees on the floor, pulling the gun safe towards her. Her hands trembled so badly it took three attempts to seat her thumb on the identification plate, with the click as it finally unlocked a welcome sound. The pistol was in her grip, checked and cocked, when another round of frame-rattling thuds came. These were accompanied by a muffled voice. "Rose, dammit, open the door."

Paul.

Heart in her throat, she shoved to her feet, stalking through the house to the front door. She peered through the tiny window to the side, verified it was indeed Paul, and unlocked the door, sliding the bolt and chain to free the door.

It swept open, and into the gap stepped the broad-shouldered frame of the man she tried to tell herself was the last person she wanted to see. But when he reached for her, ignoring the gun in her hand, and pulled her into a tight hold, she closed her eyes and gave herself over to the feeling of safety and comfort that seemed to radiate from him.

"God, Rose. I was scared to fuckin' death."

She turned her head, resting her cheek against his chest, the fast thumping of his heart directly underneath her ear.

He shuffled her backwards, and she heard the door close and lock behind him. Rose relaxed into his arms and breathed, deep and slow, the bone-deep exhaustion beginning to creep back.

"I didn't mean to worry you." She hated knowing she'd caused him distress. "I wasn't paying attention to the phone." That was truth, and he didn't need to know that at least a couple hours of that inattention had been spent in a fugue in her car.

"Scared me, baby." She felt pressure against the top of her head, and the tiny smack of lips told her it was a kiss. "I imagined all kinds of things." Rose tried to pull back, but his arms contracted, squeezing her tightly. "Lemme just have this for a minute, baby. Just this, promise."

He moved, and she felt the unmistakable press of his hard cock against her hip. She was suddenly, acutely aware her choice of pajamas tonight was a pair of boy shorts and a tank top, both thin enough for summer. Her breasts were flattened against his hard chest, and the iron grip of his arms surrounded her. "Paul, I'm okay."

"Oh, I know you are, baby. I got you right here, and that's the only thing that's gonna keep me sane." He pulled in a deep, deep breath, then blew it out slowly. "I wanna talk for a minute before you kick me to the curb." His chuckle was deep and rich, rumbling under her ear. "And I'd sure feel a mite more comfortable if you'd secure your weapon."

She realized her arms had crept around him and the butt of the pistol was digging into his back. "Sorry." She stepped backwards and he came with her, foiling her attempt to put space between them. "My gun safe's in the bedroom."

"Okay." His agreement didn't make sense until she was moving backwards, Paul steering them up the short hallway. Hers was the only open door, and he unerringly aimed for the dark opening. "You got a clapper or something?"

She chuffed a laugh at his reference to ancient technology, then called out, "House, bedroom light on." There was a low tone; then the light on her nightstand flicked on with a quiet click. "One better, as far as I'm concerned."

"I do not disagree. A clapper'd mean I had to let you go. This works in my favor." Next to the bed, he glanced down and made an approving sound. "Nice little collection. Shoulda locked the safe up after you retrieved your—" He gripped her wrist and pulled it from around him, exposing the pistol. "Oh, nice. I'm a Sig Sauer fan, too." She squatted and he crouched next to her, one arm still draped around her waist as if he couldn't bear to be separated from her. "Walther P99, too. So precious."

"Don't tell me." She unchambered the cartridge and pressed it back into the magazine before laying the gun back in its place in the safe. "You're a Glock man?"

"Guilty as charged. I got one or ten." He reached out and closed the safe, pressing the lid until it clicked and the light on the front flashed green, then amber. "Now, that talking." Paul rose to his full height and drew her up beside him. "I'm thinking the bed looks comfy. But I want you right here." He turned and sat, then pulled her between his knees. "Lemme ditch the boots and wallet, and I'll be ready to sit a spell."

It was awkward and foolish for him to work around her body to take off his boots, but he did it, not letting her out of the reach of his arms for a moment. His head brushed her breasts several times, and when she glanced down, her nipples were drawn into tight peaks not disguised by the thin fabric at all. From where he bent over, nose level with her crotch, he could probably smell her arousal, too. Still, he persisted, and only a few minutes later he was in the middle of her bed, back to the headboard, ankles crossed as he stretched his legs out.

Her fingers were twined with his, and when he tugged, she went, lying next to him. The anger and disappointment she'd been flooded with earlier was gone as if it had never happened. Rose bunched a pillow under her head and looked up to see him studying her intently.

"I know what happened." He launched into his story without preamble. "I know what you saw, and I get what it could have looked like if you weren't in possession of all the facts."

"What did I see?" The lithe blonde in his arms, her head bent backwards as he leaned close. Rose shook her head. "I saw you and her."

"You saw me and my ex-wife." He dropped that bomb and let it lie there while Rose rocked with the explosion. "Colleen and I decided before my final deployment that when I got back, we'd divorce. We married because...hell, I'm not sure either of us know why we got married. But we did, and then Erika came along, and that seemed a good reason to tough it out."

"Tough it out? That doesn't sound good."

He reached for her, fingertips trailing along the edge of her jaw. "It wasn't." His thumb slid along her bottom lip, tugging it to the side. "We weren't good to each other. My fault as much or more than hers. But by the end, it could have been ugly. The fact we were such good friends was the only saving grace."

"You're friends with your ex-wife?" She pursed her lips underneath his touch, then pressed her lips to the pad of his thumb. "That's noble. I can't stand my ex. As in, I'd walk ten miles out of my way to avoid having to piss on him if he were on fire."

Paul chuckled and shifted in the bed, sliding down and onto his side so they faced each other. "That's disturbingly specific."

"I've given it a great deal of thought." She paused, deciding whether to give him the rest of the story or not, but then figured he'd earned it many times over. "He cheated on me. I was overseas as part of OEF; at that time I was at Bagram. We were supposed to have a video call, but when it connected on his end the camera was aimed at the bed." Staring into Paul's eyes was too much, so she lowered her gaze, focused on his throat. "Our bed. That he was in with a strange woman. At least it wasn't someone I knew, right?"

"Fuck, baby. That's harsh." Paul's bent knuckles caught under her chin, lifting her face so she met his gaze again. "Lemme guess, he tried to tell you it wasn't what it seemed?" She nodded slowly. "That explains your reaction, why you didn't believe me."

"Well, I knew what I saw. And I was disappointed because I thought there was something between us. Tiny, just a little thing, but maybe, possibly something." His hand stroked down her neck, and she arched into the touch, chin lifting on a sigh. "You hugged her, and it seemed a natural thing for both of you, like you'd been with her for a long time."

"I was. We were married for a decade. Our daughter's not quite a teen now, so you can do the math. We've not been together for a long time." His fingers grazed across the top of her shoulder, pausing to play with the thin strap of her tank top. "I haven't slept with her for four years."

Rose's eyes popped open, and she stared at him, watching as his lips curled in a slow smile.

"I surprised you." She nodded. "I'll take it a step farther." He inched closer until she felt the heat from his body all along her front. "I haven't been with anyone else since then, either."

"Four years?" She shook her head in disbelief. "Surely you didn't have to be celibate. A good-looking man like you?"

"Didn't have to be, no. But bedding someone without having a connection doesn't appeal." He leaned in and hovered there, teasing, his lips a bare tantalizing breath away from hers. "I haven't felt this kind of connection before." His hand glided down her arm, thumb brushing against the side of her breast. "It's strong with you. We fit together in so many ways." The kiss started soft and slow, his mouth exploring hers, lips pressing and pulling back, the kiss renewing with every change of pressure or pace. "I've been trying to get to know you better for months."

"I wasn't sure." She slipped her arm under his, pulling herself tight to him, the heat from his erection nestled against her core. She angled her neck and looked up, watching as his eyes darkened with desire. "I kept talking myself out of it being real."

His hips thrust forward, grinding his cock against her. "It's real, Rose. So damned real."

Five

Wolf

She's everything I've ever wanted. He pushed up to an elbow, arching over Rose, who shifted to her back. Wolf slipped his fingers through her hair, straightening and arranging the locks until they were spread out over the pillows. "Woman, you're so fucking perfect." She stared up at him, lips slightly parted. "Gonna kiss you." He made good on the promise, dipping to capture her mouth again, relearning everything that pulled a reaction from her, impressing every moan, every soft sigh, and each writhing shift underneath him into his memory.

"Paul." Soft and breathless, his name was a whisper from her lips as her chin lifted, breasts pressed tight to his chest when she arched up.

"God, I like hearin' my name like that." Needy, she was so fucking needy. *For me.*

Outsiders might think this was fast, too fast. But they hadn't lived the lives of the people in this bed. She was a warrior just as much as him, and God knew he understood how quickly it could be ripped away. She probably had the same memories of her time spent deployed, and while that might not be a question he'd ask here and now, he still understood the need to move forwards. To not let grass grow underneath their feet, because it could all be gone tomorrow.

"I want." Just that, no additional explanation needed, but her simple words galvanized him into motion as, fingers to the hem of her shirt, he drew it up her body, exposing creamy skin with every inch.

"I got you, Rose." He lay his lips to her belly, drawing a line up to where the fabric had bunched under her breasts. Nudging with his nose, he gained access to the soft curves, laving the darker pebbled circles of her nipples, pulling them into his mouth and sucking firmly, teeth nipping gently at the tender flesh. She gasped out his name again, and her hands left his shoulders to cup her breasts, presenting them for his attention. He moved from one to the other, repeating the same movements, until she was unable to stay still, hips thrusting up against the weight of the thigh he'd thrown over her legs.

Wolf laid his palm over the mons of her pussy, covering her and pressing lightly. "If you don't want to be with me tonight, Rose, I need you to tell me now. I want you so damned much, baby. You don't even know what you do to me." She pushed up, thighs shifting apart to give him better access. "That's an answer, yeah, love that. But I want to hear you, baby. Want to know you're with me in this."

"Paul." Her voice was soft but firm. "Make love to me."

"Music to my ears." He lifted away, shifting to kneel beside her, leaning over to kiss her as he drew the waistband of her skimpy pajama bottoms down, taking the silky panties she wore with them. He smiled against her lips when she bent her legs, shoving with her feet to make it easier to discard the unwanted clothes. Tossing them aside, he brought the top over her head, careful as it gathered her hair to flow through the opening.

"Please." She stared up at him, eyes open wide, the green overshadowed by darkly dilated pupils. He kissed her, coming down over her body like a blanket, covering her, groaning when her legs fell apart and he slipped between them, his jeans-covered erection notching into the apex of her thighs like he'd been born to be with her. "One of us has too many clothes on."

Paul laughed at her grumbling. "True story." He kissed her deeply, tongues sliding together, twisting and tangling in the heat of her mouth. "Lemme take care of that." Her palm against his chest paused his movement, and he waited.

"Let me." She pushed at his shoulder, and he went with the suggestion, moving to his back in the middle of the bed. Naked, glorious in her confidence, she rose over him, and he gave himself over to her gladly.

She made quick work of his belt and the fastening of his jeans, careful as she drew the zipper down. She shoved them partway over his hips, just enough to get her hands on his cock. Fully erect, the crown was wet with arousal, and he groaned when she dipped her head to lap delicately at it, the tip of her tongue flicking over the slit, gathering and drinking down what she clearly saw as an offering to her.

Then she abandoned his cock. Moving to his shirt, she unbuttoned it one slow movement at a time, beginning at the bottom and spreading the tails wide, exposing him in her own way. He smiled at how they went for the same thing, using different methods, both highly effective. He tightened his abs and felt his cock jerk in response, heat from her body blazing everywhere they touched. She chased the slowly opening fabric with kisses along his belly, up a line to his chest, where she curled her fingers in the hair, making her way to his flat nipples, kissing and licking, and nipping at him. He fisted his hands in the covers on either side of his body, trying to hold back the need to take over. To flip her to her back and spread her legs, to drive deep inside.

"My control will only go so far, baby." He thought it was fair to warn her. She tipped her head so her eyes gazed up at him even as her mouth worked his flesh. "Jesus Christ, woman. You're killin' me here."

"Good way to die, yeah?" She grinned and moved back to what she'd been doing, with one addition. Heat encompassed the head of his cock. Then it was exposed to the chill in the air as her fingers curled around the shaft, stroking down to the root, where she gripped tighter.

He gasped and groaned, thrusting up into the tight fist she made around his cock, fucking into her hand. She straddled his thigh and ground her pussy against the rough fabric still covering most of his bottom half. "Kiss me, beautiful." His hands abandoned their grip on empty fabric and found their way to the back of her head. He cupped her skull with both palms, lifting her face away from his chest and bringing her up so their mouths clashed, hard and hot. The next moments were a blur of heat and pressure, wet tongues and deep kisses.

He finally maneuvered her to her back, more of an ease than a flip, still losing the heat of her hand on his cock in the process. He stretched out over her again, and she shifted, letting him slip back into the cradle of her thighs. He pressed forwards, the shaft of his cock slipping up through her lower lips easily, finding her wet and slippery. He buried his face against the column of her throat and froze. "Baby. Fuckin' drenched for me. Love that. Wanna be in there now, wanna be bare, but gotta take care of you. Lemme get a condom and lose the jeans."

"Okay." Her soft answer drifted hot across the shell of his ear, her tongue flicking and licking along the curve. The hold she'd taken on his arm and shoulders didn't lessen; she pulled him tighter than ever, even as she repeated her agreement. "Okay."

"You gotta let me go, baby." Her legs slipped over his, heels hooking along his calves and pulling him deeper into her. "Rose, that's the opposite of letting go." He chuckled when she moaned, then met her moan with a groan when her hips flexed up and slid that welcome heat against the length of his cock again. "Woman."

"I know." Her limbs squeezed tighter for a moment, then relaxed, the hand that had been curled around his bicep slipping up to cradle his cheek. "But you need to understand, I don't want to let you go. I wanna hold tight for as long as I can. I wanna be yours, Paul. I wanna be your everything."

"Fuckin' perfect for me." He reminded her with a kiss before he pushed away to kneel on the mattress again, this time between her thighs where he could take in the vision spread out before him. Red hair in a tangle of curls draped over one shoulder, full breasts on display, budded nipples standing at attention. Her soft curves dipped to her hips, her rounded belly calling for more kisses, more gentle touches, more love—and for an instant, he let himself imagine her even more rounded, full of child, a gift he didn't know he wanted until this moment. Darker red between her legs, pink lips peeking through. She moved, and he watched her breasts shift, her hips slide side to side, and he crawled off the end of the bed in a rush. Condom retrieved and applied, jeans and socks discarded on the floor, he flung his shirt towards a corner. Divested of everything that would keep him from her, he put a knee between her legs again, bringing himself back up within kissing distance of her lush lips, laying claim to her mouth as he reached between them, lining himself up with her entrance.

"It's been a while for me, too." She whispered this benediction against his lips, and he nodded even as his heart soared at the knowledge his Rose had been waiting as well.

"I'll be slow, take care of my Rose. Gotta tend to her sweet-like." The crown notched into her opening, and he pushed gently, muscles shaking as he held back, barely thrusting in and out, giving her time to stretch painlessly. "Gonna go slow as you need, baby. If it's too much, you tell me and I'll take care of you."

"It's a lot to take in." She laughed softly, and he loved hearing the sound here in her bed.

"You sayin' your man's got a big dick?" She laughed again, but it caught in the middle on a gasp as he felt the head enter her fully for the first time. Out, then in again, each movement erotic torture when all he wanted to do was slide deep, fill her on a single thrust, and love her hard.

"Is that you asking for a comp—" Her breath caught again as he pushed deeper. "—liment?"

"Perfect for me." He lifted to kiss her, then pressed his forehead to hers, staring into her eyes. "Wanna watch you take me."

"You're looking in the wrong place then, mister." He thrust, and her eyes opened wide, mouth making a tiny circle as she huffed air in. "I'm taking you down there."

"Wanna watch your face as you let me in. Never wanna forget this, Rose. Wanna think of this for always. Our first." The way her expression softened, he knew he was making inroads into whatever resistance she still held against the idea of him and her, of them, of the couple they were meant to be. "My Rose. My baby. My girl."

"Paul, it's so…" She breathed in long and slow. "So intense." He paused, thinking he might be pushing too fast, and she quickly clarified. "Not bad, honey, don't stop." Her legs spread wider, and he slipped deeper inside her on a rush, his hips jerking instinctually until he was rooted. "Oh my Jesus."

"Okay?" He held there until she relaxed underneath him, her heels hooking over his calves again. One arm curled around his waist, and he felt fingers drawing tiny circles against his flank. Her other hand threaded through the hair on the back of his head, holding them together. "Baby?"

"Yeah, honey. I'm good." She gave a tentative flex of her hips, and he groaned at the way she drew him deeper. "Oh, you like that?" She flexed again, lifting and arching her back, hips rolling against him. His cock twitched firmly, deep inside her, and this time she was the one who gasped. "Paul?"

"Mmhmm?" He kissed her hard, then glided his lips along her jaw until he lost contact with her skin, burying his face in the pillow as he concentrated on the tight clasp around his shaft, savoring the molten heat that surrounded him.

"*Move.*" Hips rolling, she tore the reins of control from him, and he started fucking into her, long slow glides of his cock from her entrance to where he fit perfectly, deep inside her.

"You're bossy." He pressed his teeth to the skin of her shoulder, holding tightly. "Did you know that?"

"You listened, didn't you?" Her nails raked a line along his spine, and he bowed into the slight pain, speeding up his thrusts to a harder pounding. "Even nonverbal instructions." She moaned and turned her head, giving him a chance to find her lips with his. "Yay."

"I can be taught." He liked the banter nearly as much as her laughter, praying it showed as deep a connection on her side as he was feeling. "Are you close, babe?"

It was her turn to abandon words, going with a humming, "Mmhmm."

"Get there. I'm right with you." Sparks flared at the base of his spine, igniting nerves leading straight to his cock and groin, his balls pulling up tight against his body. "Come on, Rose. Come all over me."

A wordless cry met his next deep thrust, and the silken grip of her inner muscles tightened, pulsing around him as she climaxed, her body going wire-tight under him, limbs contracting to clutch him close.

Paul followed her over the cliff, letting go the tenuous hold he had on himself, thrusting hard, pushing deep into her, withdrawing and renewing the connection in short, quick strokes. White pleasure blasted through him as he came, jaw clenched, head thrown back on a groan as his body stuttered to a stop and held deep. His balls throbbed, and electric pulses of ecstasy fired again and again as he filled the condom.

He pulled in a deep breath, filling his senses with Rose. Nothing but Rose. She'd become the center of his world, and he wanted to bury himself inside her again and again, never coming up for air, just the two of them on an island of her bed, staying together for the rest of their lives. The intensity of his emotions startled him but wasn't frightening. He already knew she was like no other woman he'd ever known, and finding out how explosively compatible they were in bed wasn't a surprise. He'd already been more than half in love with her. *This just sealed the deal.*

Now to convince her she felt the same.

Six

Rose

"No, I'm working tonight." She turned down his offer of dinner but grinned when Paul huffed out a disappointed sigh. "I'm off at eight o'clock, though. So not too late. Only six hours away."

"My house or yours?" The smile he wore as he laid out his expectations was clear in his voice, and the fact that she could pick up on that made her laugh softly. "What's so funny, Rose?"

"You're smiling." She shrugged, then realized he couldn't see her. "I like it."

"I am. You always make me smile, baby." A buzzer sounded in the distance, and she knew it was the bell on the customer door of his shop. "I gotta go. See you at eight. I'm cooking, so bring your appetite."

"Where?" She asked the question into dead air, Paul already having disconnected. "Hmmph." Flipping to the text application, she tapped out a quick message asking for location clarification then hit Send, shoving the device into the pocket of her apron.

Looking around the diner, she shook her head. They'd been reopened for a couple of weeks now, it having only taken a few days for the damage to be repaired. Working overtime, her memory kept overlaying the reality with remembered destruction and left her feeling unsettled. It was something she suspected Gary felt as well, their interactions having been stilted and uncomfortable. It was a little disconcerting that the perpetrators hadn't been identified or caught, but she knew the state police were keeping a closer eye on the diner now, which gave her some sense of security. She'd gathered from overhearing tiny bits of conversation Paul had with the other men in the BFMC that they were keeping watch, too. She assumed it was because she and Jenn both worked here, and both were involved with men in the club, but her mind kept returning to how Paul's position in the diner had been targeted so specifically.

She pushed through the door into the kitchen to drop off the latest order and shivered slightly as she stepped over the spot where the man had died. He'd been identified, a local man who was known to the cops because of the plethora of bad choices he'd made throughout his life. Hooking himself to the other two men had been the final one. He'd come through the back door as Gary was exiting, and they'd scuffled for a moment before Gary'd broken away. It was supposed the man who died had been assigned the flanking movement by the driver or shooter, but it hadn't worked out the way they'd intended. One of the shots through the counter had punctured the kitchen door, catching him in the belly and severing an artery in the process. He'd bled out in minutes, and when she'd asked, the cops said even if she or Paul had known what had happened, it was unlikely they could have halted the inevitable.

She hadn't suffered through flashbacks after that first night, the event having been pushed back in her consciousness by her immersion in all things Paul Bailey. Few nights had passed without his arms around her, his hold possessive even in sleep. The last time she'd declined an invitation to stay over, he'd shown up at her kitchen door at zero dark thirty, carrying a tray of coffee and pastries in apology. He'd shaken his head when she asked why, urging her to accept the offerings instead of answering. From the circles under his eyes, she suspected that like her, he hadn't slept well alone.

No matter his hints, she believed it was too soon to be thinking household consolidation. There were still too many things unknown about each other. While she knew it wasn't a mistake to be falling in love with him, she'd fought so hard to be strong on her own that it felt a little bit like giving up to be thinking of herself as part of a pair again. *But I also don't want to think about him not being part of my life.* She shook her head at her own confused musings. *Damned if I do, damned if I don't.*

"How you doin', Rose?" Gary stood in front of her, spatula in one hand, brow furrowed.

"I'm good." With a forced smile, she glanced at the back door to verify the bolt was locked. "I saw a couple of cars pulling in, wanted to give you a heads-up."

"Okay." He didn't move, just stared at her. "I didn't know what to do, okay?"

Rose frowned at him. "What?"

"When he came in the back door, there was gunfire out front already and I was freaked. All I could think about was getting away." He scrubbed across his forehead with the palm of one hand, then held that pose, keeping his face hidden from view. "I didn't think about anything else. I was scared and ran, okay? I just ran, and I didn't think about you."

"Oh, Gary. It's okay. I'm glad nothing happened to you." This wasn't the first time they'd worked together since the diner reopened, but his guilty confession explained his distant attitude. "You couldn't have done anything against them. Dale only kept the one gun under the counter, and I had that."

"Yeah, but I ran. Just ran and left you hanging." His hand dropped, and he stared at her with red-rimmed eyes. "I'm sorry, Rose. So sorry."

She stepped forwards and pulled Gary into a brief hug, holding tight as she told him the truth. "I'm glad you're safe. There's nothing to forgive." She released him, arms falling away. "No need for apologies, promise."

He ducked his head in a tiny, awkward nod, then turned back to the grill. She heard a suspicious sniff before he called over his shoulder. "Thanks, Rose."

She pushed through the door and into the front room, quickly cataloging the tables and where the patrons were in their dining experience. More drinks at table four, and the two cars she'd seen parking were just coming inside, looking at her quizzically. "Sit anywhere you want. I'll be right with you." She dealt with the drinks first, gathered dirty plates from another table, and finally made her way to where the two couples had chosen to sit, a corner booth with plenty of room to spread out. "If you're hungry, menus are on the table," she pointed out, because they hadn't yet retrieved them. "Can I start you with drinks?"

Her phone buzzed in her pocket, and she smiled, knowing it was probably Paul responding to her question.

Drink order filled, she kept busy, ringing up order totals and making change, clearing empty tables, rolling silverware for the next shift to use, and trucking back and forth to the kitchen to pick up hot dishes and deliver them to the tables.

She glanced outside, surprised to see the sunlight dimming. Déjà vu hit her hard, the surreal feeling she'd been here before. Looking around the diner, she found one couple still seated at the table Tom and Barbara had occupied the night of the shooting. There was a lone man seated in the booth where Paul had been seated. *And me and Gary.* She shook her head, shuddering as a chill worked up her spine, gooseflesh rising on her arms.

The man in the booth lifted his mug, and she nodded but held up a finger because the couple were approaching the register. Another similarity to that night. Transaction complete, she said goodnight and turned to the counter where the coffeemaker sat, quickly setting up another pot to make fresh coffee. It only took a couple of minutes, and when she turned around with the carafe in hand, the man from the booth stood in front of her, Dale's shotgun in his hands and pointed directly at her.

There was a ball cap pulled low over his forehead, but she saw the glint of his eyes as he stared at her. Shifting from foot to foot, he shoved the shotgun a couple inches towards her. "Open the register." His voice was low, and carefully modulated, almost as if he were masking something. "Now."

"Okay." She took a half step to the side, wanting to have the register drawer between them when she opened it. "I'm opening it now." They didn't have an alarm system, no magic silent button for her to push. "I'm doing what you asked." She'd lifted both hands when she'd seen the gun, the weight of the coffee carafe heavy in her hand. For an instant she considered throwing it at him, but it was unwieldy, and she didn't like the uncertainty. Out of habit, because it was nearly the end of her shift, she hit the cash out button instead of the one that would simply open the drawer. "Shit. Sorry. I hit the wrong… It'll just take a minute."

Glancing up at what she could see of his face, she saw he was blinking rapidly, pupils drawn down to a tiny circle in his eyes. He was either high or scared to death. "You're friends with that other bitch, aren't you?"

"What?"

He moved one hand up and down the slide of the shotgun in a nervous caress of the smooth wood, and she suddenly realized she hadn't heard him rack it yet. *If he pulled the trigger now, it'd be on an empty chamber.* She knew an experienced shooter could rack and shoot the five rounds waiting in the magazine in under four seconds, but he didn't strike her that way. The butt of the gun was inches away from his shoulder, which would gain him a broken bone if he pulled the trigger in that position, or gain her precious fractions of a second while he repositioned.

"That bitch. She didn't want anything to do with me, but she latched on to Blade fast. Bitch. You're friends with her, aren't you?" His chin lifted, and she saw half-moon scars along his throat. "He marked me, took her from me and fuckin' marked me."

A motorcycle entered the parking lot well away from the diner and backed into a spot she knew well. *Paul.*

With the racket the register made as it rattled off the report tape, ballcap guy hadn't noticed the sound and wasn't watching behind him, so he didn't see the moment when a sauntering Paul saw what was happening and his pace turned into a sprint, arrowed directly towards where she stood behind the register.

"Talkin' to you, bitch."

She stared at him, then without second-guessing the instinct, threw the heavy carafe filled with hot coffee directly at his head. The glass smashed into his face, breaking and spraying sharp shards mixed with hot liquid all over his head and shoulders. The ballcap went flying, and he dropped the shotgun on the counter as his hands went to his face, blood welling between his fingers. She grabbed the gun, racked a load into the chamber, and leveled the shotgun at him, butt of the gun pulled snugly to her shoulder.

Paul ran in and, without pausing, tackled the now-screaming man, carrying them both to the floor with a heavy crash.

"Gary, call the police." She raised her voice to a shout as she heard the first of several meaty thuds, Paul's fists unerringly finding their target on the would-be robber's face.

"Stop," the man cried. "You're assaulting a police officer."

Paul's head jerked back at that, and he held the man down with one fist around his neck. "Fuckin' cut. Are you kidding me?"

Gary appeared next to Rose, portable phone in hand, face pale as he spoke into the receiver. "Yes, he's contained for now. Just get here."

Rose lifted the barrel of the shotgun to the ceiling and realized somewhere in the past few seconds the register had finally stopped its infernal racket.

"I'm a cop. Get off me." The man writhed under Paul, who didn't seem disturbed by his movements at all.

"You were robbing me." She laid the shotgun on the counter and flipped the safety on. Leaning over so she could see the pair on the floor, she ignored the glass and puddles of coffee and shouted down at him, "You were *robbing* me at *gunpoint*."

"I just wanted to talk to you." His head jerked to the side as his face turned red, and she realized Paul had clamped down on his throat. "Ggargh."

"Paul, don't kill him. I wanna move in with you, honey, and that'll be kinda tough if you're in jail."

"Castle law." He didn't look up at her, using his other hand to restrain the man's wrists. "Within my rights."

"Uh, we're in a diner, not a house." The man's lips were turning purple, and when he blinked, she saw red in the sclera of his eyes. "Let up on him a little."

"You're my goddamned home. Don't matter where we are. He was threatening you." Paul angled his head so he could cut a glance up at her. "You wanna move in with me?"

"Well, your house is closer to the bike shop and I like your kitchen. Nice counters. Lots of storage. Big plus in my book." Sirens sounded in the distance. "Gary, be sure to tell them the man on top is the good guy."

"Rose Bronson, I love you." Paul looked up at her, a poignant vulnerability in his expression. Then he whipped his head back around and snarled at the still-struggling man sprawled on the floor. "Stay the fuck still, fuckwit."

Rose was still laughing when the state police swarmed through the doors.

Seven

Wolf

First man through the door was Doug Putnam, the major he'd spent time talking to when the diner had been shot up. The man took one look and didn't hesitate to hit a knee beside Wolf, with that knee directly in the middle of the asshole's chest. The cop muttered, "Got this," and Wolf handed control over, giving fuckwit's wrists a final hard twist before he released and stood up, the sweet sound of the man's sobbing breaths music to his ears.

"Rose." He rounded the end of the counter and reached for her, only relaxing enough to suck in a deep breath when he felt her arms close around him. "Jesus, baby. Scared the hell outta me." It struck him again how well they fit. She snuggled closer, and he rested his chin on top of her head, watching the cops deal with the man on the floor. If their actions and words were to be believed, they weren't tolerant of having a bad apple in their midst. "You're so damned fearless, Rose. He could have killed you."

"Nah." She shook her head, and he angled his mouth next to her ear.

"Yeah, he could have, baby. And then where'd I be?" He couldn't remember being this frightened during his entire roster of deployments overseas, even the missions that put him far behind enemy lines. "Huh? Where'd I be without you?"

"He wasn't a threat."

"Fucking hell, woman?" He stepped back, hands on her shoulders as he held her in front of him, crouching to put their eyes level. "He had a goddamned scattergun and you had a fuckin' coffeepot."

"He never racked it. The chamber was empty, Paul. I wasn't careless. It was a considered risk, and one I felt warranted in the moment." She lifted her chin. "I'm not a fainting daisy, waiting for rescue. I'm trained Security Forces, nearly seven years of overseas assignments, and I can handle myself."

"I know you can. I've seen it. Doesn't mean I'm not scared to death when it's happening right in front of me." His chest swelled with pride at how she'd responded, both with the asshat and with him just now. "I kinda dig the fact you aren't afraid to put me in my place, because you know your own worth. Proud of you, Rose." He squeezed her shoulders, slipping his hands down her arms to her hands. "I don't want to live through that again, though. Fuck, baby."

Putnam had walked over beside them, and Wolf waited for Rose to acknowledge the man before he did.

"Are you all right, Ms. Bronson?" His voice was soft and smooth, aiming at soothing, and Wolf had to hide a grin when he saw Rose zero in on the man. "This is twice now we've met under trying circumstances."

"Major Putnam." She addressed him sharply, and Wolf rocked back on his heels as he watched the wave of confusing emotions roll over the man's face. "Is that man a member of your troop?"

"Until we can officially terminate his employment, yes, ma'am." Putnam opened his mouth to say something further, but Rose cut him off.

"And what about the other man who was part of the other 'trying circumstance' under which we met?" She moved to Wolf's side, and he rested one arm across her shoulders. He knew it was a possessive hold and didn't give a shit. She cut a glance his direction then homed back in on Putnam and continued, "I think it's pretty clear your man was half of the duo who shot up the diner."

"Ma'am, with all due respect, he's not my man." Putnam shook his head without dropping his gaze. "He ceased being someone I would support or protect when he stepped inside this diner tonight with the intent of committing a crime. Right now, I don't know anything about his involvement in what happened a couple of weeks ago, but you can bet we'll be all over that. If there's a connection to be made, we'll make it."

"I hope you'll keep us updated as you can." She inclined her head, graceful as a queen acknowledging a subject. "I do understand the requirements under which you work, so I wouldn't ask you to expose your investigation to suspicion. That said, an off-the-record conversation over coffee goes a long way to rebuilding confidence."

"Ma'am, I do not disagree with you." He paused a moment, shaking his head as he gave her a tiny grin. "We'll need a statement from you. I'm happy to give you a ride if needed." He cut his eyes to Wolf, his expression growing stony. "Mr. Bailey, we'll need to talk to you, too."

"You aren't gonna like my story any better than Rose's." Wolf grinned, then directed his attention to the man being led out of the diner in handcuffs. "But I'll bet you'll like it better than his."

"I suspect we will." With a nod, Putnam turned and walked out.

"I quit."

The loud declaration came from beside them, and Wolf turned to see the cook, Gary, standing there, knuckles white around the phone in his hand.

"What?" Rose looked as confused as Wolf felt.

"I. Quit." Gary held the phone out to her and Rose took it. "This place ain't safe. Twice now, and both times I was here. This is bullshit."

"Gary." Wolf waited until the man looked away from the circus of cars and lights in the parking lot and over to where he stood with Rose. "Did you see Rose today?"

"See her smash the guy in the face with the pot? Yeah. Why?"

"You ever see that kind of badassery anywhere else? I'm thinkin' this is the safest place to work these days, with Rose on shift at least." Her shoulders started shaking, and she turned her head to bury it against his chest. "Might wanna reconsider, knowing what kind of security you have right here."

"Damn, I didn't think about that. Okay. Yeah." The man's head was nodding up and down rapidly, like a flocked chihuahua on the dashboard of a car. "Yeah. Forget the quitting thing, Rose. I'm stayin' right here."

Rose lost control of her laughter at that point, and it sounded good, right, giving him hope this wouldn't add to the weight of her nightmares going forwards. The owner walked in and, after a quick debrief from Rose and Gary, kicked them both out, saying the diner would be closed for a couple of days while he dealt with the attempted robbery.

At home later, Rose cuddled into his side as she put voice to the question Wolf had been asking himself since he'd looked through the door and seen the man with a gun pointed at his woman. Recognizing him had been secondary to getting him the fuck away from Rose and making her safe. But once the scene was controlled, he'd started watching for the second cut. Knowing the men had been joined at the hip during their whole failed time with the club, he couldn't imagine they'd broken off the toxic friendship after being dumped out. Having two shooters at the first incident had underscored his thoughts. But now this guy had acted alone, and that didn't fit the pattern.

"Wonder where the other guy was. I kept waiting for him to pop out like a prairie dog from a hole." Her hand went from splayed flat on his chest to a tight fist. "Gary's religious about making sure the back door is locked now, so there was no access from that side."

"Putnam will find out." Wolf had a lot of faith in the man, cop or not. "He promised to get to the bottom of it, and the man's motivated."

"The whole troop is motivated." She harrumphed softly. "This gives them a pretty ugly black eye. I heard one of the troopers say he was on duty, too."

"So I assaulted a police officer out of uniform, while he was robbing a diner, on his shift? I hit the jackpot." Rose's fist slowly relaxed, and she took up drawing tiny circles in his chest hair. "Had to be scary, having him point the gun at you."

"No lie, it was." Her frame shuddered, and he gave her a reassuring squeeze. "I turned around and he'd leaned over the counter, already had the shotgun in his hands. All I could think about was getting him out of there without anyone getting hurt. Then—" She laughed softly. "I got mad. In my gut I was calm and steady. Years of training kicked in, you know?"

Wolf made a sound of agreement, not wanting to interrupt the flow of her talking. She needed to get it out, so it didn't stay stuck inside and fester. An emotional debrief was just as needed as the situational ones.

"But underneath that, man, was I pissed. It went from zero to a hundred in a breath. How dare he, you know? I'm just working, a job I chose specifically because it had little chance of putting me in that exact position. So I'm working, and this stomped turd comes in and wrecks that little place of security I had."

Her voice had thickened, and it sounded like tears were close to the surface. He hated hearing it but couldn't do anything except be there for her. Wolf soothed a hand gently over her hip and side, down then up. Slow and steady.

"And there he was, a threat that I knew in my gut I could neutralize. You were active in tense situations, so I know you understand the split-second decisions."

"Yeah." Until he spoke, Wolf didn't realize he was fighting tears, too. Her pain was so raw, it ripped a hole inside him. "Do-or-die moments."

"Exactly. But underneath it, I was so pissed. I mean, I'm still pissed." She rolled slightly, turning into him and lifting up on her elbow. "I saw you coming, storming across the lot and into the diner like an avenging angel, and I was glad you were there. But it scared me, Paul." Her trembling lips pressed into a bloodless line for a moment as her throat worked to swallow. "I can't lose you."

"You're not gonna, baby." Both his arms closed around her, and he pulled her tight to him. "You can't get rid of me that easy."

"The look on your face." Her tongue dipped out and wet her lips, leaving them glistening and demanding a kiss. He waited, understanding she needed to finish this. "I thought you were going to kill him."

"I would have if you hadn't stopped me." He shook his head in a short arc. "No question. The man had a gun on the woman I love more than breath. He doesn't deserve to still be this side of the sod."

She leaned a little closer, brow furrowed as she hissed, "I wanted you to. I wanted to. Why is he so fixated on the diner?"

"You realize he's one of the shitstains that threatened Jenn?" She nodded. "You know he was trying to be a Freak?" She nodded again, the lines in her forehead smoothing out. "I suspect he focused on the diner because that's where he lost his chance to be a member. That's all. He's fixated on me because I'm the one who gave him a beatout when we cut him and his buddy. Problem is he didn't take the lesson offered. He's turned it into some kind of sick vendetta instead."

"Beatout?" Her chin moved to the side when she said the word, tentatively, softly, like she was trying the idea out in her head.

"Man disrespected the patch he was being offered a chance to earn. He did that in a way that took away that chance. As a club, we don't take things like that lightly." He studied her face for any glimpse into what she was thinking, but her expression was carefully neutral, which gave away more than she probably wanted. "There's no in-between there. No room for discussion. Man is either in, or he's out. He was out. My job was to drop a warning he couldn't mistake that not only was he out, but even out he needed to respect the patch and keep his distance. He's proven himself lacking in the ability to comprehend a simple message. A poor student."

"So it's a way to police yourselves?" Wolf shrugged, his gaze attentively on her expression, glad to see it thoughtful instead of horrified. "I think I can understand that. All groups have the same controls; some are less brutal but also less effective." She lay on his chest, cheek nestled between his pecs. "I'm glad you're okay."

"I'm glad you're okay, too." He let it sit for a few minutes, her breathing slowing but the movement of her hand on his chest signaling the lack of true rest. "You want to move in?"

"I'm your home?" She answered him question for question, and he grinned.

"I want you here or there. Anywhere, Rose. If you didn't want to leave your place, I'd be there in a heartbeat." He reached for her chin, tipping her face up to study her expression. "I just want you, full stop."

"Same." The smile she gave him was blinding, and he offered up a silent prayer of thanks that she'd listened to him and processed the information in a way that allowed him to still have this in his arms.

"I'll call the brothers. We'll move you tomorrow."

Her head jerked back and she frowned again, this time in confusion. "It doesn't have to be tomorrow."

"Are you fuckin' kiddin' me right now?" He flipped her to her back, rolling and stretching out over her, giving a twist of his hips so he fell between her legs. "I'm not givin' you a goddamned chance in hell to back out of this deal, woman." A simple lip press turned into a soft kiss, which morphed naturally into one that was deep, wet, and long, the slow glide of tongues swelling into panting heat. "Wanna love on you, Rose."

"I'm yours."

Her simple declaration touched something deep inside him, and he closed his eyes as the almost painful resonance flowed through him. *She loves me*. Still marveling at that miracle, he kissed her again, only pulling back when her lips were swollen, cheeks and chin red from his beard, and her eyes filled with stars.

Eight

Rose

He leaned over her, staring into her eyes, an intense expression on his face she couldn't place. He'd been different since they'd gotten home after the events at the diner. *Home*, she thought, and knew a tiny smile broke through when the corners of Paul's eyes crinkled, and he asked with a rumble of laughter, "What was that?"

"I just realized you're my home, too. I don't care where we are either, as long as I'm with you."

He snorted softly. "Brownnoser. You're just sayin' that 'cause you're sweet on me."

His eyes crinkled more when she gave him a broad smile, and she loved the fact that her joy was reflected in his own. "Guilty as charged, sir."

Paul dipped his mouth to hers in a slow, wet kiss that gave as much as it took, the sweet feeling of his lips giving her tingles through her body. He cradled her head in his hands, fingers threaded through her hair when he pulled back, staring at her with a quirked eyebrow she already knew meant trouble.

"Hey."

"Hey back atcha." Rose turned her head and pressed a kiss against his palm.

"I've been wondering something."

"Only way to find out is to ask." She kept her face angled away, unease building in her gut. Something told her she didn't want to be looking at him when he asked whatever this was.

"You were a cop in the military." She shrugged and kissed his hand again, closing her eyes. "A specialized cop, with a fuckton of training the local yokels can't even dream about. Highly trained, you're clearly good at your job. What are you doin' pretending to be a waitress?"

She opened her eyes on a slow blink and stared at him, trying to find a way to stall answering, or maybe derail the conversation entirely. This wasn't something she'd shared often, or easily, and yet, here they were.

"Rose, what's goin' on in that head of yours?" He brushed his nose against hers, the movement hypnotic, soothing. "Tell me, honey."

"I was good." Her lids dipped closed, mouth getting ahead of whatever her brain had planned. "Good enough we were a requested semi-permanent attachment to my Marines." She huffed out a breath, not finding any humor in the possessive statement. "Those boys were everything to me. I may have worn a different uniform, but we were family."

"I know how that is. The kind of connection forged by fire." His big palm cupped her cheek, warm, a connection she didn't realize she'd needed.

"I lost three of my boys. I'm not at liberty to talk about what happened except in very broad, general terms, but it was a mess, Wolf. What a fucking, fucking mess." She blinked wet from her eyes, something that happened every time she remembered that day, the bodies slung in the back of the recon vehicle, the frantic calls over the radio for help that never came. "My tour ended, it was time to re-up, and I declined. I took the out, separated, and never looked back."

"Was it preventable?" His question surprised her, and Rose held his gaze for a moment before giving him a single slow nod. "By you?"

"Twenty-twenty hindsight...yeah." Lips pressed together, she steadied her voice before continuing, hating how it fractured around the words. "Something was off that day. I couldn't put my finger on it, at least not until a couple of weeks later, after I'd been released from the hospital."

"What happened to you?" His palm slipped to her throat, to her shoulder, and down her side. Fingers tensing at her waist, he restated his question. "The injuries weren't enough to pull your contract?"

"Broke some ribs, punctured a lung." She laid her hand over his, then brought his fingers to the dip between her ribs, placing his fingertip over the fading scar. "Drainage tube." He explored that section of skin for a moment; then she carried his hand farther up, pressing it flat over her side where she knew the bump was. "That's the bad actor that went pokin' around inside me."

"You see any lasting issues?" His voice was almost clinical, and she huffed her amusement at him. "What?"

"I forget sometimes, that you get it. You know, you understand probably better than anyone else I know. One of my boys was AF, not Marines. He was our counter for when we came under attack." He shifted, and his hand covered her breast, palming it gently. "When snipers attack, you beat 'em back." Rose blinked, surprised at the wet still in her eyes. "So yeah, I think it was preventable. If I'd paid attention to the tiny group of locals just outside the gates, I would have seen what was missing."

"It was old men and women, wasn't it?"

She smiled at his astute summary of a situation he couldn't have known about unless he'd lived it, too. "Give that man a cigar. All the fighters were waiting for the signal about what route we'd be using. They used the kids as runners to pass the info."

"Were you in love with him?"

Rose froze, every cell in her body pausing for a split second while she took in the impossible ask Paul had made. "Wh-what?"

"The counter sniper. You were lovers." She didn't know what to do with his statement, something so clearly not a question, as if it were a foregone conclusion and known fact. "But were you in love with him?"

Rose shoved at Paul's chest, trying to move him off her, but only succeeded in sliding herself sideways. She did it again, using strength this time, intent on levering him away. He settled heavily over her, arms coming around to slip under her shoulders, holding on tightly.

"Get off, Paul. This isn't funny."

"Why'd you give up SF?" His face hovered just over hers, eyes boring into her.

"Let me up." Her arms were trapped against her sides, but her legs were free, and she planted a foot in the bed, rolling them to their sides. "Paul, come on. Let go."

"If I let go, are you getting out of bed?" When she didn't answer, he sighed, touching his forehead to hers. "Rose, I love you. Hard stuff or not, I love you. Someone as driven as you are won't drop a lifetime's career for nothing. It had to be big, and losing people would do it. But losing someone you're posted with, that's more of everything. I know it is. I've lived it. I've lived having to crawl across pieces of my friend to get to safety, because he didn't make it." He blinked, and she saw the thinnest circle of blue around his wide pupils. "Shit like that digs deep. I know. Now…" He adjusted his grip, relaxing his hold, giving her more freedom when she didn't immediately bolt. "Did you love him?"

"No. We were friends, but with benefits. He was funny and easy to be around, and the perfect place to land after a long, stressful day. But there wasn't any…" She fumbled for the words. "I didn't love him." She waited a beat for the censure she expected, surprised when it didn't materialize. "I wished I did. After. You know?" Paul made a sound she took to be agreement. "He shouldn't have even been with us. His mission was to protect the flight line. We'd had a sniper taking steady shots at the equipment for days, and Wilson was supposed to be zeroing in on the guy. But we were headed into a district normally closed to us, because the locals policed the area themselves. When Wilson heard where we were going, he didn't let up. Dog with a bone."

"The district, was it hot?"

"Paul, the whole area around the base was hot. That was one of the reasons they'd pulled us up that far."

"So was it hotter than hot?" Rose rolled her eyes. "I'm just tryin' to get a sense of it. I want to understand."

"Yeah, it was a different level of tension whenever we even skirted the zone. Going in?" She shivered and crowded closer to his body. "We had to be on our game for sure."

"What happened?" She'd opened her mouth to remind him of the restrictions when he seemed to realize his question verged on those topics. "As much as you can share, what went wrong?"

"I didn't read the situation. I should have picked up on the changes and aborted the mission entirely." Rose wiped her palms on the sheets. "No matter what happened or didn't happen, it comes back to that was my role, and I failed. When I failed, people died."

"No offense, but did you have that kind of power? Not my experience when we had SF attached, but maybe your posting was different." The sheets rustling spoke of his movement, so she wasn't surprised when his leg wrapped around hers, dragging her closer. "They had input, sure, but aborting or staying the course wasn't up to them."

"We had a very collaborative relationship." Rose closed her eyes and sighed. "What are you getting at, Paul? What's the purpose of this interrogation?"

"Baby, ain't an interrogation. I'm tryin' to lay a path to what I see and have you walk it beside me."

"What do you see, then? Say it plain, because I'm tired and...I just want to be done with this." His lips pressed to her forehead, and Rose smiled. "Please?"

"You're takin' responsibility for things that weren't under your control for one, and feeling guilty because the decisions of others caused the death of someone you cared for." Once again, she opened her mouth only to have him forestall her words. "I know you didn't love him. But I know my Rose. She wouldn't be close to someone without being close to them. Even without the heart involved, my Rose would only want the best for that person."

She nodded, because he'd spoken truth about Wilson. "I can't stop feeling guilty when I know if I'd read the situation and spoken up, they'd have listened to me."

"How'd your ribs get broken like that?" His fingers skated along her side, something that should have been a tickle, but it was done with such care it felt comforting instead.

"IED on the other side of the truck. It blew the vehicle sideways and into me, knocking me about forty feet back. The impact was what injured me."

"Quit the diner. Soon as you can."

Rose blinked in confusion, unsure how he'd gotten to that conclusion from the conversation about her injuries. "What?" Unless he meant it because he felt she was unsafe? "Because of tonight? I get the sense that was more about his connection with your club than the diner. It's not a dangerous place to work, Paul."

"Rose, you're meant to be a cop. Protect folks from bad guys. You're wasting your talents slinging hash and coffee." His brows drew together. "It should freak me out, suggesting you take on a job where you could be killed, but after seeing you in two different situations, I know deep in my gut you've got what it takes. Better'n me, so it's a good thing I turned to workin' on bikes instead of law."

"Could I do it? Sure." She rolled to face away from Paul, snuggling back against him as he wrapped his arms around her. "When I got out, though, the last thing I wanted to think about was being put back into a situation where I could fail someone. As a waitress, the worst I can do is fluff up someone's order, and if I do, there's always a chance for a take two. Or three, if it's really an off day." She adjusted against him again, smiling when he wedged a thick thigh between her legs. "Pretty blameless."

"So for you, it was either all the responsibility or none?" Rose stiffened. She hadn't thought about it like that. "Serious lack of in-between there, darlin'. Life and death, or eggs over easy instead of scrambled."

She didn't respond, and they lay like that, twined together in the middle of the bed until his breathing had slowed, deepening. Out of the darkness, his voice rumbled, vibrating against her back.

"So if not then, how about now? You got enough time between you and that shitstorm back in the sand to make a different pick?" His hand swept across until it settled on top of hers where she clutched the edge of the pillow. He cradled her hand in his, fingers threading between. "So fuckin' smart and capable. You're the whole goddamned package, Rose."

"Go to sleep, honey."

"Okay, but promise you'll put some thought into it, yeah?"

She turned her head into the pillow to hide her smile even though he couldn't see it. *Persistent man.*

"I promise."

***

Wolf

"Brother." Wolf's extended hand was clasped tightly by Gibby, his whole body yanked forwards into a one-armed clinch. "Good to see you, man."

"And you." Gibby gave him a final thud against the patch on his back, then released him, tipping his head back and shouting through the clubhouse, "The Wolf-man is in the house, my brothers. It's a rare occurrence these days." Wolf shook his head with a grin as Gibby told the prospect behind the counter that served as a bar, "Shots, FNG. Line 'em up, man. Shots all around."

That set the tone for the next handful of minutes, as men Wolf knew and trusted beyond breath clustered around him. They ribbed him about his absence, speculating amongst themselves for the reasons, each raunchier than the next. He held his peace throughout, because their words held respect for Rose without exception. After a second round of shots on his tab, he peeled away from most of the men, sidling up alongside Gibby where he stood next to the wall.

"Gibby, I wanted to talk to you." One of the things he'd always liked about Gibby was how straight the man spoke, no beating around the bush or waffling, and he knew Gibby valued the same from his men. "In private, if you can give that to me."

"You got it." Easy as that, they were walking through the noisy clusters of men and into the office at the front of the building. Gibby swept an invitation with a wide-swung arm, then pulled the door shut behind them. "What's up, Wolf-man?"

"Putnam talk to you about anything?" Gibby's headshake wasn't surprising, but it was disappointing. "Shit."

"Don't mean I haven't activated other resources, brother." Leaning far back in his chair, Gibby swung his legs up and propped his feet on the edge of the desk. "After the initial shoot-'em-up at the diner, I started asking around, dug up a little dirt on our former friends."

Wolf knew it wasn't worth his breath to ask why they hadn't done that before things came to this pass, because he had been part of the officers meeting that changed the bylaws after their second run-in with the prospects-gone-wrong. Founded decades ago, the bylaws had reflected the mindset of the time. Now updated, hangarounds had to submit to a background check before things progressed from there, with each step along the way laid out in black and white. No more loopholes for FNGs to slip through.

"Do tell? I'd love to know more." He tipped his beer up and took a sip, waiting.

"FNG in the wind is the stepbrother of Gregory Popova, mob boss in Birmingham. Word is Popova cut the asshole loose from any mob back up months ago, just about when he showed up on our patch. My understanding is when we branded those boys with our Fuck No, he went crying back home and got run out of town on a rail a second time." Gibby was referencing a previous situation when the two former prospects had threatened Blade's woman and had been caught and taught a painful lesson. They'd branded the men with the club's initials followed by a circle with a slash across it. Not just a no, but a fuck no. An irrefutable way for other clubs to identify them as ill-fitting men for the life. "That's when the FNGs decided to fast-track their trooper training. Three months instead of six, and fuck if I know how they managed that shit." Gibby lifted the bottle in his hand and drained his beer in a few hard pulls. "For now, the one man is in custody and looks to be getting lost in a morass of red tape. They might never get him to trial for anything at this rate."

Wolf sighed in frustration. "That shit. I wish I'd just fuckin' killed him there in the diner."

"Your woman was right to talk you into stopping, and you know it, man." Gibby's knowing eyes drilled into him, seeing far too much. "You and I both know it. Wouldn't matter you killed him with your fists, all the prosecutor would have had to hear was what you did back in the day, and he'd be all over that shit."

"If it drags out too long, do we have options?" Wolf finished his beer, setting the bottle on the desk next to Gibby's empty. "Just askin' what's possible, you know?"

"Anything's possible, if the pockets are deep enough." Gibby grinned broadly. "I got deep pockets, my brother. We'll deal with what needs dealt with."

"Obliged, Prez." He stood as Gibby did, rounding the desk and reaching out. This time he was the one who pulled Gibby into a clinch, and as he pounded the man's back, he muttered, "Love you, man. Freaks forever."

LACK OF IN-BETWEEN

94

Nine

Wolf

Connecting the call with a tap of his finger on the phone's screen, he lifted it to his ear with a smile for Rose. She looked over her shoulder at him, rolling her eyes at his expression and going back to what she'd been doing. She was busy at the stove, two pans going, one with eggs and one frying bacon and sausage.

"Yeah?"

He hadn't noticed who was calling, so wasn't expecting his ex-wife's voice. "Paul?"

"You got me. What's up Colleen?" Staring at Rose, he didn't miss the way her shoulders stiffened at his ex's name. They'd talked the subject to death as far as he was concerned, and he trusted Rose to know he wasn't interested in Colleen, had nothing to do with her outside of their daughter's needs. "It's early."

"It is not. I waited until after ten to call." Colleen was laughing, and he blew out a breath that had caught in his lungs, fear always a visitor when she called out of the blue. "I wanted to let you know the daddy/daughter dance is next weekend."

"A father and daughter dance?" Rose turned half around, head tipped to the side, and he watched as a tiny smile curled the corners of her mouth. *Wanna kiss that off you, baby*. His dick started to take notice, and he quickly turned his attention back to the phone. "When and where? You know I'm on it if Erika wants to go."

"It's Saturday evening, there's a dinner before the dance, and everything ends by eight o'clock. She'll need flowers, but I can get those if you want." He heard noises in the background, shouted laughter ending in a splash. "Or you can pick something up. Let me know."

"Kids in the pool?" Rose's smile had grown as her expression softened. He walked to her and slipped an arm around her waist, dropping a kiss against her temple.

"Yeah, Temple and Masters are trying to beat Erika in a cannonball contest." The fondness in Colleen's voice didn't discriminate between her three children. No matter they had two fathers among the kids, she loved them all.

"You're a good momma, Colleen." Tipping his chin to his neck, he watched as Rose flipped bacon, using the spatula to stir the scrambled eggs.

"Thank you, Paul. You're not a half-bad dad yourself."

God, I'm glad we figured out how to be friends through this. Life would have been a hell of a lot harder if they didn't get along.

"How about this idea. I'll pick her up at noon, and we'll go for lunch. I'll take that chance to introduce her to Rose, my girlfriend. If they want to, they can girly it up that afternoon, and I'll bring her back in time for you to help her get dressed. Erika can pick out the wrist corsage she wants that way, make it match her nails or whatever." Rose had gone board stiff in his hold, and he angled his head to look at her face. Longing was mixed with fear, but the need, the desire for what he'd talked about was there, and that emotion was strong. "And if you're okay with it, she can stay here Saturday night. I know it's not my weekend, but things have been jumbled and I haven't had her in too long."

"I know our vacation messed with the schedule, Paul. We appreciate you being so flexible. Of course she can stay with you. As often and as long as you want." Colleen, her husband, and all three kids had taken an end-of-summer vacation, traveling to the coast and over into Florida for two weeks. The weekends leading up to their vacation, Erika'd had plans with friends, so that meant he'd only had Erika a couple of times since he'd started seeing Rose. Both of those had been on weekends Rose worked, and it hadn't been a good time to do the introductions. Erika knew he was dating and had been supportive when he told her it was getting serious. Her exact words were, "About time, Daddy. I don't like you being alone." *God, I love my girl.*

"No problem, Colleen. Let me know if she's cool with the plan, and I'll execute on my end."

Colleen laughed softly, the sound nearly lost in the splashes from the kids in the pool. "Ever the military man."

"I stick with what I'm good at." Rose glanced at the cabinet, and he released her and opened it, bringing down a couple of plates at her approving nod. "Gonna go. Tell my girl I love her."

"Will do. Talk soon."

He laid the phone on the counter and turned back to Rose, bracketing her in on both sides with his arms braced against the counter. He brushed her hair aside with his nose and pressed a line of softly possessive kisses along the nape of her neck. "You okay, baby?"

"You're cute when you're in daddy mode." He didn't have to see her face to know she was smiling, and that earned her a nip at the juncture of neck and shoulder. She shivered, and he grinned against her skin. "So." Her shoulders rose with a deep breath. "A daddy and daughter dance, huh? I want pictures."

"You heard me talkin' to Colleen. What'd you think about what I said?" His lips brushed against another warm patch of skin that he grazed gently with his teeth, following with a sucking kiss. "You down for a day with my little girl?"

"For you?" She turned in his arms and lifted her chin. He dipped to touch his mouth to hers. "Totally ready for some girly time, if she's okay with it."

"She likes to see her old man happy. Erika's a smart kid. She knows her mom's happier married to her stepdad than she'd have been with me, and she knows I wouldn't have been happy at all. I don't know how much she remembers from before, but if she even remembers a little, it's too much. We weren't kind to each other when things were falling apart." He stared into Rose's eyes, willing her to understand and believe. "She's gonna see what this is between us, and she'll be on board. I guarantee."

It turned out he was right. Erika not only was okay with having lunch with the two of them, but the idea of doing mani-pedis with Rose had her giggling into the phone later that evening. When he disconnected from that call, he caught another soft, sweet expression on Rose's face that he liked a lot. He'd seen it off and on all day as he and his closest brothers in the BFMC had packed up her house and shifted all her stuff either to his home, now theirs, or into a storage unit he already rented. He hadn't realized most of her furniture was leased until a truck showed up to take it away.

Wolf loved knowing that from now on, wherever he called home, Rose would be there.

The day of the dance dawned, and he hung the dark gray suit he owned on the closet door to take a lint brush to it. Rose walked in and studied him for a minute, then asked, "Not your dress uniform?"

He cut a glance at her to see if she was joking but found a puzzled look instead. "No, I'm not up to regulations and not likely to shave." He lifted a hand to rub the thickening beard across his jaw, then threaded it through his hair, back to front, letting the longer, curly strands settle behind his ears. "Nor am I willing to cut my hair. So civvies it is."

"Did you have a military wedding?"

Wolf turned to face Rose, placing the lint brush on the dresser as he walked towards her. "Nope. Was a big affair, and she wanted the groom and groomsmen in tuxes. It didn't bother me either way." Hands on Rose's hips, he swayed them back and forth in time to the music she'd left playing in the living room. "Shoulda been a sign, I suspect."

"Well, whatever you wear, I know you're going to be an escort Erika will be proud of." Rose laced her fingers behind his neck, pressing her lower half closer as he started shuffling his feet, leading her into a slow dance. "Is it weird that I'm crazy nervous to meet her?"

"I'd worry more if you didn't give a shit. Be like that long-ago wedding where I didn't care about any of it except how long it would take to get through." He bumped his nose against her cheek, turning her face so he could kiss her softly. "Go ahead with your bad self." Another kiss. "Give all the shits."

"Okay." She returned the caress, dancing her tongue across his lips in a way that made him groan. Rose pulled back, a sparkle in her green eyes. "Consider them given." She stilled, and using her hands on his shoulders for balance, rose on her toes so they were nearly eye to eye. "I love you, Paul."

Wolf held her gaze for a long moment, then fell on her, crowding her backwards against the wall, pressing close all along her body as he kissed her deeply, mouth working across hers, licking and biting. She arched against the hard surface behind her, breasts pushing against his chest. He pressed his lips in a series of tender caresses along her jaw, and she offered him her throat with a soft whimper he took as invitation.

"Get naked." He knew his tone was an order, expected her to snap out of the haze she looked to be in and set him to rights, but she just nodded, her hair moving against his face as she stretched her arms overhead, shirt disappearing from in front of him. That barrier gone, he moved to her breasts, lifting them from the bra and laving first one nipple, then the other, with the flat of his tongue. Mouth tight against her, he drew her deep into his mouth, barely registering when her bra went away as he moved to her other breast.

Under his hands at her waist, he felt her jeans loosen, and he slipped his fingers down, inside her panties and over her ass, shoving at the fabric as he went. A moment later she was naked in front of him, and he took a knee in front of her, pushing his nose deep into the cleft between her legs, lapping and licking. He found her clit and drew his bottom teeth across it, then pursed his lips around it and sucked. Her stance widened, giving him more room, and her hands landed on his head.

Over the next few minutes, using that hold, she yanked and pulled, guided him where it felt best, and then stilled for a moment before shuddering hard. Her voice quaked in a way he'd become addicted to as she called his name when she came.

Wolf wiped his mouth as he stood and freed his cock. He only took the time to shove his jeans down far enough to allow for freedom. Running a hand over her hip, he reached down behind her leg and lifted, supporting her knee until it rested on his hip. Hand wrapped around the shaft, he guided the head of his cock between her legs and sank inside on a long, slow thrust that made them both groan.

"Oh my Jesus." Rose's whisper came as he rolled his hips the slightest amount. "Good God." Her hands landed on his chest as he pulled back, then pushed inside again. Fingers plucking at the fabric, she muttered, "You have clothes on. Why are you still dressed? Take your shirt off." He ignored her soft command and rolled his hips one more time, grinding deep and staying there, feeling her pussy fluttering in pulses around him. "Oh, Paul."

"Finally, she realizes who's fuckin' her." Rose's eyes snapped open, and she focused on him, a frown drawing her brows together before he pulled out nearly to the tip. Her eyes opened wide, mouth making a tiny "O" of displeasure at the move. He stalled any complaints with a heartfelt, "I love you, too, Rose."

As he spoke her name, Wolf fucked into her hard, pounding her against the wall. He took possession of her mouth with a brutal, demanding kiss that renewed, again and again, her breaths coming in quick gusts of air panted against his lips. The sound of skin slapping against skin filled the room, and a picture on the wall next to Rose's head wobbled, teetering on the edge of the nail holding it up. Rose reached sideways and propped one hand on the dresser, her other one winding around his neck for support.

Wolf looked down between them and saw his bare cock appearing and disappearing, hard and glistening from her wet. The vision of her taking him ungloved, the sounds of her tiny gasps and clasp of her hand, the way her pussy pulled him deep and held tight—it would be only minutes before he'd be too far gone to stop. *She's mine. Any kid we make is gonna be loved*. He had visions in flashing pictures in his mind: Rose swollen with his baby; Rose nursing their child; a stumbling toddler's hands wrapped around his fingers. His cock throbbed and he plunged, hips rolling. She was an inferno of heat all around his cock as his balls and nerves buzzed and hummed, electricity thrumming just under his skin.

He came hard, in a toe-curling and vision-whiting rush, dimly aware of Rose's nails digging sparks of blissful pain into his neck, her head buried against his chest as she sobbed out her own orgasm. Through the waves of pleasure, he told her, "Love you. Fuckin' love you. God, Rose. So much."

Knees locked so his trembling legs didn't deposit them ignominiously on the floor, he stayed with Rose, leaned into her, one arm propped against the wall, his other hand traveling a possessive trail from her lower back, around the curve of her ass, and down to her bent knee, still hooked over his hip. By the time his breathing had steadied, his cock had softened and he slowly pulled out. "Rose, look at me."

She tipped her head back and gave him a view of her gorgeous face. Pupils blown, she gazed at him with a soft and sated expression, her lips puffy from his kisses. He dipped back in for another taste, sipping from her lips with gentle, caressing touches. Raising up an inch or two, he studied her for a moment before telling her, "You get pregnant, I wouldn't be displeased." Her breathing stuttered and paused for seconds, until he felt compelled to remind her, "Breathe, baby." Mouth closed, she pulled in a breath, nostrils flaring cutely.

"It's the wrong time of month." Her whispered words pierced him with a bloodless wound, and he set that aside for now. Time enough to dissect that emotion later. "I'm not looking to be a mom anytime soon, but if we have an accident it's good to know we're on the same page."

Paul took a deep breath and released a surprising amount of tension. He might not have minded if she got pregnant, but it would have put an indefinite pause to any changes in a career path for her. "Yeah, it is." He unhooked her knee, letting her leg fall in a controlled drop to the floor. She hissed, and he suspected pins and needles were making the renewed blood flow known. "Shower with me. I wanna take care of you, Rose."

Eyelids dipping briefly, she looked away from him and then back, cheeks slightly flushed. "I'd like that."

"Then that's what we'll do."

Three hours later he stood at Colleen's front door, hand raised to knock, when the door opened underneath his hand and he had an armful of Erika.

"Daddy."

"Daddy's baby girl. You ready for lunch, shug?" Her head moved against his chest in a nod, and he smiled as he dipped to press a kiss to the crown of her hair. "I'm thinkin' that Italian place. Sound good?" Another nod, then she gave his waist a squeeze before backing away a step and gifting him with a wide smile.

"Where's Rose?" She angled her head and looked around him. "Oh, I see her." Then she was gone, tearing away at a run towards the truck where Rose stood next to the passenger door. Erika stopped just in front of her and said something Wolf couldn't hear; then Rose's neck tipped down and she put her face close to his daughter's, responding. Then the two people he loved most came together in a world-righting hug. He stood still and watched, giving them space to explore a budding relationship he was determined would last a lifetime. Rose's arms were folded tenderly around his girl, and she stood with one cheek pressed to the top of Erika's head.

"I'd say you're going to have a good time."

Wolf glanced over his shoulder to find Colleen standing in the doorway. "Yeah, I'd agree." She gave him a quick smile as she closed the door. He appreciated her instinct to not impose on this moment for Rose and Erika when he turned back to see them already arranging themselves in the truck, where his daughter would be sandwiched by the two adults.

That'd give her full range of the radio. *Fuck*. He still smiled broadly as he made his way to the truck.

The afternoon was a running sequence of those kind of moments. His girls laughing at Wolf's reaction to Erika's song selections. Watching as they bent their heads together over the menu at the restaurant, Rose explaining a couple of the choices. At the salon, Erika more confident than he'd ever seen her, picking out colors for Rose to wear on her nails.

Then things went sideways.

Wolf had stepped out of the salon and over to a coffee shop a couple of doors down. When he came back, he noticed Rose looked alert, her attention focused on two girls who'd taken their seats in the pedicure chairs. Erika's head was down as she attempted to pretend to study the color being layered on her nails, but the way her shoulders were pulled up told him the pose was just that, a way to camouflage whatever she was feeling.

Before he could say or do anything, before he could even approach, Rose stood out of her chair, lifting one finger to the girl prepping her color on the other side of the narrow table. As she moved towards the two girls, he sped up and had just gotten close enough to overhear when she lit into them.

"If I ever hear you talking about my girl like that again, I'll have your butts in a sling faster than you'll know what hit you." Head lifted high, Rose was tall enough to look down on the girls where they sat in the elevated chairs. "I know both your mommas, and they would be mortified to know you were turning into mean girls. If you think for one minute that kind of behavior will get you anywhere except ostracized, then you'd better take another stab at thinking." She flung one hand out towards the rest of the salon. "See all those people watching this go down?" Neither of the girls moved; they sat frozen, eyes wide and locked on Rose. "I won't even have to tell anyone anything. They'll make up a story and it'll be talk of the town by nightfall." She stepped closer to them, and he closed the distance, putting his hand on her back as she hissed, "Erika is sweet and kind, and if you don't want that in a friend, fine. But there's no way you can justify being so ugly to her. Shame on you."

Rose whirled and then stutter-stepped as her gaze landed on him, and he watched as she willed away the angry tears gathering in her eyes.

"I love you more." He saw her chin wobble at his words and shook his head, lifting a bent knuckle to steady it. "None of that now. You're a momma bear when riled up. Momma bears don't cry."

"They do if someone's hurting their babies." Rose rolled up on her toes and brushed a chaste, sweet kiss across his lips. Voice lowered to a whisper, she told him, "They were quiet, and she didn't hear what they said, but the way she acted when they walked in told me enough. All I did was put a little fear into them."

"My Rose." He kissed the tip of her nose and stepped back, guiding her back towards the manicurist's station. "Finish getting girlied-up."

Lying in bed with Rose that night, a dance-exhausted Erika under the same roof, Wolf felt settled, filled with a peaceful contentment he hadn't felt in a long time.

Rose twisted around in his arms, turning to rest her head against his chest, auburn hair in a cloud across the pillows. He tangled their legs together, clasped her hand in his, brought it up between them, and fell asleep.

Ten

Rose

The ringing phone first registered as a sound in her dream, a fuzzy scene that splintered as she heard Paul's sleep-roughened voice answer, "Yeah?"

He grunted in response to the humming voice she heard on the other end of the call, and then the air in the room changed, vibrating with energy.

Rose twisted to lie on her back, reaching out to trace the curving lines of Paul's back as he leaned up on one arm, the other holding the phone. The covers had puddled at his waist, and she slipped her palm up the broad expanse of skin available to her. Muscles shifted under his skin as he leaned back into her touch, telling her without words it was welcome.

Abruptly he lurched upright, moving away from her with legs swinging off the side of the bed as he barked, "The fuck you say?" The vibration she'd felt a moment ago was eclipsed by angry energy rolling off him. "How in the hell did something like that happen?"

He was silent a moment, and she again heard the buzz of whoever was on the other end of that call. She slipped closer, curling around Paul's back until she could rest her head on his thigh. One of his hands dropped to her head, and she felt his fingers begin to thread through her locks, slowly and softly, as he had a hundred times since they'd been together. She'd woken up to him playing with her hair more than once, and the man's fixation seemed to be working in his favor this time as she watched him take a deep breath and visibly calm himself.

When he spoke again, he was no less angry but sounded less like he wanted to murder someone.

"So what you're sayin' is he's in the wind, and you've already turned over the rocks you know about to find him, but you're comin' up blank?" Silence from the caller, and Paul grunted, then spat, "I find him first, you'll never know." That stirred up the conversation, and she overheard pieces of shouted words. "Nope. No premeditated anything, I'm just informing you that if I find him first, you'll never get to stop lookin' for him. You know what I did, so you know I'm not boasting when I say that."

He didn't wait for any additional rejoinders, disconnecting the call and tossing the device to land on his nightstand with a rattle. His chin dipped, and he stared down at her for a long moment, fingers moving in long sweeps from the top of her head down her neck. A muscle in his jaw ticked, and then he gave her shoulder a gentle nudge. "I gotta pee, baby. I'll be right back." She watched him gather up the phone as she moved towards the middle of the bed, saw his sideways glance at her as he disappeared into the bathroom, and then stared as the bathroom door slowly closed, settling into place in the frame with a quiet click.

LACK OF IN-BETWEEN

Eleven

Wolf

After texting an alert to the club's officers, Wolf took a moment to stare at himself in the mirror. Eyes clear, chin high, he showed no fear and would suffer no regrets if things went down the way he hoped. If the cops caught the asshole, then he'd leave it up to the law. If they didn't, he'd own the man for threatening Rose. No other way to do this, not and be the man he was.

Shaking the tension from his arms, he palmed the phone and turned the light off before opening the door, intent on not disturbing Rose any more than she had been by the call. He needn't have bothered.

Seated on the foot of the bed, legs folded underneath her, she kept her gaze on him as he made his way the short distance to her.

"Couldn't go back to sleep?" He murmured the question against her mouth when he bent to kiss her, the softness of her lips calling him like a siren. She hummed a response, and he wrapped a hand around the back of her head, drawing her up for another firm press of his mouth to hers.

When he made to pull away, her palms cradled his cheeks, holding him still. Her thumbs brushed across his cheeks, up his temples, across his mouth still damp from tasting her.

"Putnam called me, too."

Fucking asshole.

Her eyes narrowed. "What are you going to do?"

This answer didn't have to be censored. She'd lobbed him an easy pitch to start. "Keep my family safe. Beginning to the end, that's what I'll do."

Lines that had appeared between her brows smoothed out, and darkness he hadn't realized was edging her eyes receded. "That'll do." Her eyes shifted side to side, taking in his whole face and expression. Whatever she saw there must have sealed the deal for her, because she visibly relaxed. "I love you."

"That's it? No 'Don't go off half-cocked, Wolf.' No 'Don't do anything stupid, Wolf.' Nothing like that?"

Her laughter rang through the room like bells, musical tones lifting and falling as she released her hold on his face and fell backwards onto the bed, hands up to cover her face.

"What's so funny?"

"You're one of the most methodical men I know, Paul. There's nothing about you that says half-cocked or stupid." She propped up on an elbow and smiled up at him. "And yeah, that's it. I trust you to not do anything that would take you away from me or from Erika. I trust you."

"I'll work every fucking day to be worthy of that, baby." Crawling up the mattress to his pillow, he discarded the phone and turned back to hook his hands under her arms. Dragging her up and on top of him, he savored the erotic slide of her all along his front, and by the time he had her within kissing distance, his dick had woken up to take an interest in the goings-on. "Because I love you, too."

116

Twelve

Wolf, one year later

Head back, he stared up into the sunlight filtering through the tree leaves. One long, deep breath followed another until, a few agonizing minutes later, he realized his heart rate had finally slowed down, gradually calming in the deceptively peaceful, bucolic setting.

Movement in the periphery of his vision kept him as informed as he needed to be about what his brothers were doing, and with his back to a broad tree trunk, it meant when Neptune approached, it had to be from the side, so the man couldn't take him by surprise as he more often did.

Wolf looked at his friend and brother, waiting. The slow shake of Neptune's head took only a fraction of a second to splinter his hard-won control. Over Neptune's shoulder he saw the narrow country lane was still empty of traffic, but that wouldn't last much longer. He could already see the red and blue strobes arrowing through the woods.

"We got any idea how they did this?" He shifted and looked to the side, at the body stretched out on the ground. The differences in the scene from when they'd gotten here were knee prints pressed deep into the heel-churned ground and the severed rope dangling from a low-hung limb. Blade had been the one to cut Gibby down, perched on Wolf's shoulders with Neptune's knife in hand. There'd been a dozen men latched on to whatever they could touch of their president, supporting his body so it didn't offensively tumble in a free fall but was carried to the ground with grace and reverence.

"I reached out to some of my buds. Couple of 'em have ways of getting me info, so I should have copies of his phone records quickly. But we may never know what lured him out here." Neptune's features were set in stone, carved in frozen granite, so he spoke through barely parted lips. This death was ravaging them all, but Wolf knew Neptune had been closest to Gibby, the two men bonding over their shared military experiences, albeit more than a decade apart in serving.

"Cops are here." He watched the three official cars pull into the clearing, kept his gaze fixed on the middle vehicle. There was a profile inside that he knew by heart, having traced it with lips and fingers a thousand times over the past year. "Oh, man. This is gonna kill her."

Gibby was a favorite of Rose's. She and the old man had spent hours talking once she found out he'd been an old-school military police during his twelve years of service. They shared ideas and frustrations, and when she'd decided to go for an opening in Putnam's troop, Gibby had been the first one of his brothers encouraging her. After Wolf, of course.

The men standing in clumps shuffled around the tree and instinctively created a rough line, the body of their president laid at their feet. Shoulder to shoulder with their brothers, they formed an impenetrable wall of support and love. Monk stood to Wolf's left, Blade and Neptune to his right.

As Putnam, Rose, and the rest of the man's troopers snapped hats into place and walked through the brittle grass towards where the men stood, Wolf watched the pain of recognition flit across her face. Then like the damned stubborn woman she was, Rose set that aside and slipped back into the officer of the law role she'd worked hard to achieve.

He understood. There'd be time enough for talk later.

Putnam asked the usual questions about how they'd been tipped off, what that tip-off had looked like, sounded like, why they'd followed up on it the way they had. Who'd been first to the clearing, who'd touched the body.

At that mention of their president, Blade barked out his disagreement, "Not a body. That's Gibby. That's my brother."

Rose's chin dipped, and she took a half step backwards. Wolf ached to help as he watched her struggle to hold on to her composure in the face of Blade's pain.

The coroner showed a couple of hours later and loaded their brother onto a stretcher with care, nervously casting glances at the scowling faces surrounding him. To his credit, he'd placed a spotless white blanket around Gibby as if he were a parent tucking his favorite child into bed. As he pulled out of the clearing and onto the dirt lane, the men of the Borderline Freaks MC walked as a single unit to their motorcycles, parked off to the side until now.

Wolf gave Rose a chin lift, and she answered with a tiny tip of her head.

He knew she understood.

There would be time for grieving, mourning, and telling tales of the fallen.

But now? This was time to plan vengeance.

~~~
~~~

THANK YOU SO MUCH FOR READING
Lack of In-between!

This story is book #3 in the Borderline Freaks MC series, and is best enjoyed as a prelude to the final installment in the series, book #4, *See You in Valhalla*. After the way the characters left us hanging in this story, I know you won't want to wait to read where Neptune and the guys take the club going forwards.

ABOUT THE AUTHOR

Raised in the south, *Wall Street Journal* & *USA TODAY* bestselling author MariaLisa learned about the magic of books at an early age. Every summer, she would spend hours in the local library, devouring books of every genre. Self-described as a book-a-holic, she says "I've always loved to read, but then I discovered writing, and found I adored that, too. For reading...if nothing else is available, I've been known to read the back of the cereal box."

Want sneak peeks into what she's working on, or to chat with other readers about her books? Join the Facebook group! **bit.ly/deMora-FB-group**

deMora's got a spam-free newsletter list she'd love to have you join, too: **bit.ly/mldemora-newsletter**

~~~~~
~~~~~

Borderline Freaks MC series

This series is comprised of four stories, and are best read in order to avoid spoilery situations.

Service and Sacrifice

"Thank you for your service" is what we're taught to say to military men and women in gratitude for our freedoms won at their expense. Less often do we thank their families, those left behind to hold down the fort, to manage the day-to-day struggle of keeping everything up in the air until their loved one returns.

When you can't count on anyone else to save you, there's only one real choice.

Amanda lost her husband to war. Alex lost part of himself. Through a series of glancing encounters, Amanda and Alex find reasons to continue on. And together, they'll discover hope and peace can be found in the most unexpected of places.

books2read.com/serviceandsacrifice

~~~

More Than Enough

When a man sees himself as damaged, imperfect, and flawed, it's hard to believe there could be love in his future. After a near-fatal accident stripped Blade of his confidence, he didn't hold out much hope … for anything.
~~~

Until Jenn—gorgeous, sweet, and kind—dropped into his life.

Where he sees destruction, she sees perfection.

Where he sees helplessness, she sees courage.

Where he sees ruin, she sees strength.

Can he ever believe he's more than enough?

books2read.com/morethanenough

~~~

Lack of In-between

Wolf finds Rose harbors more secrets than he expected, and the deeper he pulls her into his life, the more he likes it.

Once a man's been embedded in the bloody aftermath of battle after battle, with no relief in sight, he's forever changed.

Wolf came home from overseas to find his world askew. He was no longer a husband, since he and his ex agreed they were better friends than partners. But he still held the coveted position of father, an experience so confusing and rewarding it sometimes left him breathless.
~~~

He's got a lot on his plate personally, and even more with the Borderline Freaks and the challenges he and his club brothers have hit lately.

He just doesn't have time to make room for a relationship.

Right?

books2read.com/lackofinbetween

~~~

See You in Valhalla

This is Angelo Dobbs' worst nightmare. A good man lies dead, and with their president and founding member gone, the leadership position within the Borderline Freaks MC falls to him.

It's not that he can't manage the easy task of leading a group of good men; he would just have preferred to stay a little farther out of the spotlight. But, when his brothers issue the call, he answers.

Carly Gibson, daughter of his dead friend, is an unexpected—but not unwelcome—complication for his new role. She's the most intriguing woman he's ever met, capable and filled with a strength of character. He finds himself instinctively drawn to her. Could he have found the woman meant to complete him, finally?
~~~

Over the past couple of years, Dobbs, Neptune to the men of the BFMC, has watched as his closest friends found their soulmates. Now, their women are an integral part of the club, and when they and Carly are threatened, Neptune will do anything to ensure their safety—and just maybe, his future.

books2read.com/seeyouinvalhalla

Other Motorcycle Club Romance Series

My Rebel Wayfarers MC and the Neither This Nor That MC series do cross over, along with the Occupy Yourself band books, so readers have a couple of choices. The series can be read independently beginning with RWMC, OYBS, and then NTNT without too many spoilers. There's also a crossover between my RWMC world and Lila Rose's Hawks MC world. Or they can be read intertwined—in chronological order.

Here's the recommended reading order if you want to follow according to timing:

Mica, RWMC #1

A Sweet & Merry Christmas, RWMC #1.5

Slate, RWMC #2

Bear, RWMC #3

Born Into Trouble, OYBS #1

Jase, RWMC #4

Gunny, RWMC #5

Mason, RWMC #6

Hoss, RWMC #7

This Is the Route of Twisted Pain, NTNT #1

Harddrive Holidays, RWMC #7.5

Duck, RWMC #8

Biker Chick Campout, RWMC #8.5

Watcher, RWMC #9

Treading the Traitor's Path: Out Bad, NTNT #2

Living Without, Lila Rose's Hawks MC: Caroline Springs #4

Shelter My Heart, NTNT #3

A Kiss to Keep You, RWMC #9.25

Gun Totin' Annie, RWMC #9.5

Secret Santa, RWMC #9.75

Trapped by Fate on Reckless Roads, NTNT #4

Bones, RWMC #10

Gunny's Pups, RWMC #10.25

Not Even A Mouse, RWMC #10.75

Road Runner's Ride, RWMC #12.5

Never Settle, RWMC #10.5

Fury, RWMC #11

Christmas Doings, RWMC #11.25

Gypsy's Lady, RWMC #11.5

Thunderstruck, NTNT #5

Going Down Easy

No Man's Land

Cassie, RWMC #12

~~~~~
~~~~~

Also by MariaLisa deMora

Neither This Nor That MC romance series

Legends are born from moments like these. Folktales spun around a single point in time so perfect, you can almost hear the click resonating through the universe as things align. Meet Twisted, Po'Boy, Retro, and Ragman, good old boys from southern states who have many things in common. First, is a bone-deep love of the biker lifestyle. Second, would be their love of the brotherhood, and knowing that you trust the man at your back. Finally, these men have the love of a good woman. None of these come without a price, and it is our pleasure to journey along with them as they discover the blessings that can be won, and lost along the way.

This is the Route of Twisted Pain
Treading the Traitor's Path: Out Bad
Shelter My Heart
Trapped by Fate on Reckless Roads
Thunderstruck

Twisted is one of the most original and interesting characters I have read in a long time. Marialisa's character building is setting a high bar for her to follow, she will hopefully continue with Po'Boy's story. The Route of Twisted Pain was pure brilliance, and I highly recommend this read.
~Penny T.

This book obsessed me!
This may be the best book I read all year.
These people...they're not characters, they're real... have stuck in my head from the day I met them.
MariaLisa deMora can throw words down that'll Twist (hehe) your insides up till you can't breathe for waiting to hear what's next!
I'm working my way through her other 'families' and yup...she really is that good.
~DeLane

Treading the Traitor's Path: Out Bad

"Treading the Traitor's Path: Out Bad is a solidly engrossing, well-written novel by a talented author.
MariaLisa deMora delivers a thrilling ride filled with exciting suspense, deliciously explicit, vivid sex scenes, and gritty, fast-paced action. Her characters are smart, complex, and strong with sharp edges. The settings meticulously detailed.
Fans of Motorcycle Club romance stories will not want to miss this second installment in deMora's exciting series."
~ NY Literary Magazine

Book Hangover

What an amazing read! DeMora does not simply wrote a book, she pulls you into a different world. When you read her work, you are very much surrounded by the characters and setting. Prepare for a book hangover because once you finish the book, you will still be stuck with Po Boy.

~KW

More More More

THIS WAS AMAZING. Highly recommend for a good story line, interesting characters. I just wish there was more more more.

~Laura

Loved This Book!

What did I just read?! Is my kindle still working? I'm pretty sure it combusted into flames while reading this story. RED HOT READ for 2017. Not what I was expecting at all! I tend to stay away from ménage a trois, because for me it's hard to say there's any kind of conflict except for jealousy, and the ending kind of leaves things unresolved and unrealistic. NOT THIS BOOK! The best one out there guaranteed.

~Linda A

So Freaking Good

...seriously this series is just WTF so freaking good. Dark, Twisted, harsh, painful and raw. Po'Boy lives for his club, his brothers and his family, there is nothing he wouldn't do for them.

~Fay

The author delivers a 5-STAR READ
I live and breathe for books like this! Fabulously Naughty!...Wickedly Hot! This is my first book by MariaLisa deMora and it will not be my last. MariaLisa delivered a 5 STAR READ! The plot is filled with action, suspense, romance and tons of hot scenes.
~Jenny F
~~~~~
~~~~~

Alace Sweets, a dark romantic suspense standalone

A dark thriller, this book is not a light read. Filled with edge-of-your-seat suspense, this intense story commands the reader's attention as it drives towards the explosive ending. Alace Sweets is a vigilante serial killer, with everything that implies and is sure to trip all your triggers. Be ready.

At seventeen, Alace Sweets turned a corner in her life, taking the wrong shortcut home from school.

Resisting the harsh knowledge her attackers will never be made to pay for their actions, Alace takes a stand. Justice must be served, and if fate's scales are out of balance, she's determined to set things right as best she can.

When the laws of men fail, the rules of Alace prevail.

5-Star Reviews for Alace Sweets

"Whatever deep dark trench [deMora] pulled a character like Alace from should be revisited again and often."
~Confessions of a Serial Reader

"deMora has a superb story-line and exceptional character development. All of her characters have such depth that will intrigue the reader..."
~Turning Another Page

"Hot, sweet, dark thriller."
~Beth D

"It will keep you on the edge of your seat and give you chills."
~Escape Reality Book Blog

"Disturbing, haunting, sickly; yet hot, sexy and heart racing!"
~Amanda L

"From the first page [deMora] pulls you into the world she has created and you do not even try to escape..."
~Little Shop of Readers Blog

"A must read for all those dark, gritty romance fans out there."
~Sweet & Spicy Reads

"You will find yourself so drawn into the story that the outside world is blocked out and your locking the doors and turning on all the lights."
~Danena F

"Don't judge me for bonding with a vigilante serial killer, she's more than what she does."
~iScream Books

"Thrilling...chilling...full of suspense, nail biting edge of your seat excitement."
~Tracey H

"Every time MariaLisa deMora picks up her pen (or opens her computer), she creates characters you want to believe in."
~Gail S

"Intriguing dark storyline, beautiful love story and nail-biting conclusion, what more could a reader ask for?"
~Manda M

"This book takes you a dark and twisted ride that is gripping..."
~Renee Entress' Blog

"This book is dark and gritty and I literally had to take a day off from reading it because it's that intense."
~My Girlfriend's Couch

"This is my favourite book so far from this author ... I recommend this book if you enjoy dark romantic thrillers."
~Cheekypee Reads and Reviews

"There's not enough stars to give this book and 5 just doesn't really do it justice!"
~DeLane C

"I couldn't put this book down from page one! Tried to stop & go to bed but couldn't sleep thinking about Alace and got up & finished the book."
~Debbie M

"MariaLisa DeMora, wordsmith that she is, made this a
story of the enlightenment of a woman and finding love
in a life where she has had none."
~Kat W


~~~~~
~~~~~

Hard Focus, a criminal thriller standalone

This is an intense page-turner, a gut-punch twist-filled story about a woman who has confidence in herself, believes she's a good judge of character, and has filled her life with people she can trust. She's right, but she's also very, very wrong. Readers will have a time of it trying to decide who to watch closest.

Where do you place your trust when your own instincts betray you?

Connie Rowe is a receptionist at a respected legal firm. She's a little bit sassy, a lotta bit happy, has good friends, and is adored by her neighbors.

Life is good.

She's got a boyfriend she enjoys spending time with. He can be a little intense, but he's got a lot going on in his own life, sorting out his young daughter and nightmare of an ex.

Life is grand.

"Trust your gut." That's what Connie's police officer father told her often, training his daughter to believe in herself through the years.

But … what happens when you can't? When your intuition lies?

What happens when things come into Hard Focus?

5-Star Reviews for Hard Focus

"Hard Focus is one very well-written tale. 5 stars is not enough for me."
~Tabitha

"What a powerful story. [deMora] kept me invested from the first word to the last."
~Jesse R

"[deMora] has a certain magical touch to writing her characters, that they become either your nemesis, your best friend, or your love interest. That is certainly portrayed in this spin around. Loved it, loved it, loved it."
~Sandy K

"I strongly recommend this book for both entertainment and to broaden your knowledge of certain laws that must be revisited."
~Words Turn Me On

"An intense page turner. Once you start, you can't put the book down."
~Tracey H

"A beautifully written, powerful read that I can't rate highly enough. This story will stay with me always."
~Gayle

"This book had twists I didn't see coming. Loved it!"
~Lori R

"Wow! I am in awe of deMora's skill in crafting this story."
~Kat W

"I keep sayin that there just aren't enough stars to give to some of Marialisa deMora's books...this one is no different!"
~DeLane

"Where do I start with this one...I read this in 3 1/2 hours uninterrupted, I absolutely could NOT put it down. Very deep, keeps you guessing, what's gonna happen next, kind of book. I love how strong her characters are, especially the females!"
~Wendy I

"Sometimes I feel like MariaLisa deMora is the one I should be watching out for. I started reading her books because I'm addicted to MC Romance, but then she decides to change things up and I just follow her wherever she leads me like a Pied Piper. I never know what to expect, and sometimes I'm afraid to find out, but it's always an adventure."
~Rosa for iScream Books Blog

"A plot full of twists and turns, a story that's not quite what it seems, strong characterization, jaw dropping revelations... what more do you need from a book?"
~Manda M

"This book kept me turning the pages wondering what was going to happen. I am usually pretty good at guessing twists but not with this book. She totally surprised me and brought me out of my funk. 5 stars."
~Glenna M

"What an amazing story! Filled with a smidge of suspense, a dash of action and a heap of realism of our country's laws and how their vague application to victims can adversely affect its citizens and the people in their lives."
~Naughty Mom Story Time

ADDITIONAL SERIES AND BOOKS

Please note that books in a series frequently feature characters from additional books within that series. If series books are read out of order, readers will twig to spoilers for the other books, so going back to read the skipped titles won't have the same angsty reveals.

Rebel Wayfarers MC series:

Mica, #1
A Sweet & Merry Christmas, #1.5
Slate, #2
Bear, #3
Jase, #4
Gunny, #5
Mason, #6
Hoss, #7
Harddrive Holidays, #7.5
Duck, #8
Biker Chick Campout, #8.5
Watcher, #9
A Kiss to Keep You, #9.25
Gun Totin' Annie, #9.5
Secret Santa, #9.75
Bones, #10
Gunny's Pups, #10.25
Never Settle, #10.5
Not Even A Mouse, #10.75
Fury, #11
Christmas Doings, #11.25
Gypsy's Lady, #11.5
Cassie, #12
Road Runner's Ride, #12.5

Occupy Yourself band series:

Born Into Trouble, #1
Grace In Motion, #2 (TBD)
What They Say, #3 (TBD)

Neither This, Nor That MC series:

This Is the Route Of Twisted Pain, #1
Treading the Traitor's Path: Out Bad, #2
Shelter My Heart, #3
Trapped by Fate on Reckless Roads, #4
Thunderstruck, #5

**Rebel Wayfarers & Incoherent MC
(NTNT) crossover stories:**

Going Down Easy
No Man's Land

Mayhan Bucklers MC series:

Most Rikki-Tik, #1
Mad Minute, #2
Pucker Factor, #3
Boocoo Dinky Dau, #4 (TBD)

Borderline Freaks MC series:

Service and Sacrifice, #1
More Than Enough, #2
Lack of In-between, #3
See You in Valhalla, #4

If You Could Change One Thing:
Tangled Fates Stories

There Are Limits, #1
Rules Are Rules, #2
The Gray Zone, #3

Other Books:

With My Whole Heart
Bet On Us
Alace Sweets
Seeking Worthy Pursuits (TBD)
Hard Focus
Dirty Bitches MC: Season 3

More information available at **mldemora.com**.

www.ingramcontent.com/pod-product-compliance
Lightning Source LLC
Chambersburg PA
CBHW050539190726
48284CB00003B/1131